THE CRUSADER: BOOK V

THE CRUSADER

Book V:
SALADIN'S SPY

by John Cleve

Grove Press, Inc., New York

First Black Cat Edition 1986
First Printing 1986
ISBN: 0-394-62129-8
Library of Congress Catalog Card Number: 85-81176

Manufactured in the United States of America

Grove Press, Inc.
196 West Houston Street
New York, N.Y. 10014

DEDICATED

TO ALL THOSE READERS

WHO HAVE KEPT GUY KINGSAVER ALIVE

FOR 793 YEARS

AND ESPECIALLY FOR

THE PAST TEN!

God does not care. That is what life means, and that's what death is. Death is something that just happens. I shall LIVE! I shall live every day, all my life, and if it is short, then . . . I shall have BEEN here!

GUY KINGSAVER OF MESSARIA,
THE CRUSADER

CONTENTS

THE CRUSADER: BOOK V

"The two powerful military orders played a considerable part in the history of the Frankish kingdom, principally because of the number of soldiers they provided. . . . The proportion of Hospitallers and Templars killed in battle was much higher than that of lay knights. . . . In a fight, their military virtues made every man of them worth two ordinary combatants, and furthermore these elite troops did not have to be paid."

—ZOÉ OLDENBOURG, *The Crusades*

Prologue

The long sandy hill lay shimmering sleepily in the Syrian sun. Its aura was of peace, of sleepy tranquility mirrored in the hawk that circled on lazily drifting air currents.

Tranquility fled when the horse exploded atop the ridge in a violent lunge. Its dashing hooves sent a few small stones and clods of earth tumbling down amid little puffs of yellowish dust. The animal was sweat-drenched, so that it shone a sleek red-brown in the hot sunlight of Palestine. Startled and affronted, the hawk flapped its wings hard, several times, and fled away to the west.

The horse did not pause atop the hill. Urged on by its anxious rider, it lunged into a reckless descent of the long slope on the hillside facing the craggy d'Entremont Castle; Krak d'Entremont, on the opposite hill. The wiry animal's mane fluttered and its tail, almost black, streamed out in the same way as the long hair of its rider. Lunging, slipping, dropping its haunches to maintain balance, the horse descended precipitately. More puffs of sandy dust rose to become a yellowish plume that trailed back up the incline. The rider glanced back in a swirl of long chestnut hair, as if fearfully seeking pursuit.

None was in sight. Yet pursuers were coming. The rider slapped the reins and dug in both heels, which were bare. Dust billowed and stones leaped up from gouging hooves to roll and bound down to the valley. Clumps of earth and scrubby grass were torn out to fly into the air and fall dead.

Some few rolled and slid in the animal's wake.

Atop the crenellated wall of the castle atop the opposite hill, a helmeted man paused and thrust out his neck to peer through the space between two merlons like the teeth of some beast of fable. He squinted.

"Baldwin! Look over there—what do you see?"

His fellow sentry peered, also squinting, through another crenel.

"Sweaty horse—been running. Rider's taking a real chance, coming down that hill so fast! Must be terrified—by'r Lady! Brother Rigord! Be that a *woman?*"

"So I think," Rigord snapped while rapidly nodding, "and unless my eyes fail me in this accursed sun, she is naked as a plucked bird for the table!"

"And being chased, I'll wager," Brother Baldwin said. He continued to watch the presumed fugitive while amid a jingling of his coat of linked chain, his fellow lookout raced to sound the alarm.

As it turned out, Rigord had not far to speed. The man in charge of the d'Entremont fortress, called Master of the Castle rather than Abbot, was just ascending to the roof for some reason never to be remembered. In moments Master Aimar was also peering through the toothy defense wall topping the castle.

The rider was indeed there, trailing dust in a plume of sickly yellow. Of the rider Aimar could see only pale skin and flying brown hair. A woman? He thought so, although at this distance and from this height it was not quite possible to be sure. Aimar had not so much as seen a woman for over a year. A fugitive, nonetheless. And no Saracen, man or maid, possessed skin so pale.

"Holy Cross of our Savior—fleeing naked! From what or whom—"

Aimar broke off to stare, for his murmured question was answered even as his lips formed the words. A flashing

4

helmet topped the rise above and behind the fugitive; the spiked helm of the enemy. The Saracen warrior's horse, too, gleamed with sweat. Aimar saw the Turk call out and point down the long hill. Then he was starting his descent; and here came another, and another, bright Turkish pennons streaming in yellow and blues and orange and greens from their lances, and Aimar was swinging from the walls to bawl out orders while Rigord went racing to make certain they were heard and understood.

The fighting monks of Castle d'Entremont began to mobilize with a discipline and crisp efficiency that was nigh incredible.

Surmounting the tall hill two sides of which were sheer and unscalable precipices, the fortress of Entremont was one of the presumed permanent outposts of Christianity in this unchristian land called Holy. D'Entremont had been raised nearly a century ago, as a hospital for those Christians of the First Crusade. Those Benedictine monks and former knights who manned it formed a new order: the Knights of the Hospital of Saint John of Jerusalem. Soon they were known as the Hospitallers of St. John. Every man of their number took solemn vows of poverty, chastity, and unquestioning obedience to God and His earthly representative, the Master of the Order. By the Year of Our Lord 1113, the Pope in Rome had proclaimed them an autonomous order. They were subject to no order and no king, and indeed only to God's representative on earth himself: Holy Father Pope.

Over the years they had become esteemed fighters respected by Turks and Franks alike. As the Knights Hospitallers evolved to be more warriors than nurses, their fortress grew to be less the hospital and more a strategic outpost essential to the continued western presence here in the east.

Now the leader of the Third Crusade of Holy Mother Church, Ricart Rex of the English, called Richard of the

5

Lion's heart, deemed the fortress essential not only to the presence of his army, but to its safety.

Aye, he had visited here, though he had not long tarried. It was a strange and solemn place that made the warrior king less than comfortable. Every barefoot resident wore a long, roughly spun robe of jet black, bearing a white cross over the heart. Yet King Richard had seen them too in their battle armor, leggings and coats of quintuply linked chain similar to his mail and that of the knights of his crusading army. Rather than sun-reflecting white surcoats, however, the Hospitallers dramatically proved their mettle by topping their armor with long-skirted surcoats of scarlet, each with a white cross emblazoned on the breast. A scarlet mantle displayed the same white cross on the shoulder. The cross was the eight-pointed one unique to the Order, resembling four notched elongated triangles set point to point. Red was surely an unwise choice of color for surcoats and capes: any dark color absorbed the rays of the sun and its dreadful heat. The Hospitallers seemed neither to care nor to notice.

Iron men, King Richard Lion-heart called them. Dreadful foes, his enemy Lord Sultan Saladin called them.

Both kings knew whereof they spoke. Both had seen the Hospitallers fight. None had seen them so much as question an order, or eat aught save their own thick nourishing bread, or quench their thirst with other than water. None had seen them have aught to do with the fair sex. The Hospitallers knew not the meaning of lust or even desire. They did not even use nuns to slake their bodily needs, as did so many of the clerics of Europe. Iron men, indeed, the fighting monks of the Order of St. John.

And now they mobilized with a speed almost astonishing at the command of Master Aimar, and soon the great gate of Castle d'Entremont was swinging wide. Iron-shod hooves drummed on the bridge across the toothy-bottomed moat. Out into the sunlight burst a party of a half-score men in

6

red cloth and dark steel. They bestrode superb war-steeds they had bred themselves, mingling a strain of Arabian horse with the bigger animals of Europe long bred and trained for the bearing of mailed knights in all their weight.

Heavy, fire-hardened lances thrust wickedly out before the men in scarlet, couched and braced in saddle-cups. Unornamented hilts rose at their left sides. The cross-shapes stood above long broad swords of steel. The sun glinted dully on blued steel and black armor, flashed as if angrily off their helmets and the bosses of the shields slung on their left arms. Their mounts gained speed as they swung down the road that led down and down from their lonely looming castle of dun-colored stone. Soon their hooves became a pounding roar along the road that wound down the steep incline in a double-S system of curves. The skirts of their surcoats fluttered in the breeze of their own passage, and short cloaks or capes streamed back in blazes of scarlet.

"God and Saint John!" their bellowing voices rose, and down they raced, at the gallop. The cavalry of the Cross of Calvary, each worth ten or more stout foot-soldiers.

From the high wall Master Aimar looked down upon that magnificent charge. He heard their voices, and knew that the Saracens on the opposite slope heard, too, so that they must look and see that now they had more to deal with than a helplessly fleeing, unmailed and indeed unclothed fugitive.

Aimar had counted their number; they too were ten, under fluttering pennons in as many colors.

Their quarry had reached the foot of that hill and was charging across the valley, crossing the great supply road, and urging the sweat-streaming roan to commence an ascent of the Hill of Saint John. Still they pursued amid flowing pennons, descending almost as pell-mell as their prey: the knights of Salah-ad-Din the Sultan; the soldiers of Allah, in their flashing silvered mail.

7

No one offered a wager as to whether they would continue and join battle or break off the pursuit, for the Hospitallers of St. John did not wager.

Then Aimar the Unsmiling leaned out through the crenellation and bellowed in his best voice: *"God and Saint Johnnnnn!"*

Every charging knight of his order raised high his lance and bellowed out the same words in reply. Reply, and challenge to the Turks.

"For God and Saint Johnnnn!"

They had thundered to the first of four tight U-shaped curves and swept around it and on, ever descending, to the second curve, and along the straight stretch beyond. Descending at speed. The hill was steep; too steep for a road to run straight down. And now the rider they intended to rescue was on that same road, urging her horse on toward the first lower curve. *Her* horse, yes; it was clear to all now that it was a western woman the Saracens chased, and an entirely naked woman at that, poor creature.

Despite the greater weight their horses bore, the crimson-clad Hospitallers raced toward her faster than she toward them, for they were on the descent and on fresh horses, while hers was sweat-covered and winded.

She saw them then; they thundered toward her like a mailed wall all abristle with the spikes of their long, long lances. Coming four abreast, they took up nearly all the hillside road. Their leader lifted his shield-arm and shouted a command; man after man drew rein a bit so that the eleven horses formed into twos rather than continue in fours. The space they left was on their right, against the hill. The fugitive's horse was more than willing to obey her tugs at its reins. It came to a halt against the hillside.

The knights of the Hospital galloped past amid dust and furious noise, and the watching woman saw that not one of them so much as glanced at her.

8

This, she thought, *may well be your greatest challenge, m'girl!*

Then they had passed and were gone, leaving behind only their dust. She decided to hold her position and await their return. She twitched the rein a bit, so that her panting mount took the few steps that enabled her to look into the dust, downslope after those monkish knights or knightly monks.

Brother Baldwin and the Master watched too, from atop the wall.

"Those Saracens will come on," Baldwin said. "Ah, had I not been on sentry duty this day! Such a battle there will be!"

"Then consider yourself fortunate to have such a vantage point from which to view 'such a battle,' Brother—and remind me to assign ye penance for questioning your duty assignment this day. But ye have wasted your breath on it, Brother. Those Saracen are ten, and they see that ten of our own ride to meet them. Think ye truly that they are so stupid, the unbelieving Turks?" Almost, the grim-faced Master of the Castle smiled; almost. "Nay, Brother Baldwin. Ten of us against ten of them is no fair odds for them, and they know it as well as we. Were there twenty of them, they might consider risking combat..."

The Turks began their curve ere they reached the foot of the other hill. Each man leaned far to the left, uphill, to ease the turning of horses still on the slope and at near-gallop. They turned onto the valley road and clapped heels to mounts, to race eastward, back around the hill they had just descended and back into the arms of their sultan. Oh, they yelled insults and imprecations, but on the run. For they were running. As Aimar had said, these ten had no stomach to meet an equal number of Franks. The Hospitallers of Castle d'Entremont were respected, and with very good reason.

9

Those men shouted their insults, too, as they came pounding down toward the road.

Aimar chuckled drily, without smiling. "Sound the recall. Our brethren would only have to slow at the foot of the hill, then make the sharp turn to follow lighter-armed men with their destriers already at full lope. We do not serve God and maintain His fortress by chasing phantoms—or fleeing infidels whose compatriots may be waiting in force just around the hill."

The men at the foot of St. John's Hill were indeed about to set off in pursuit, when the horn sounded high above. With none of the grumbling less disciplined and godly men might have made, they reined in and turned their mounts' faces back toward the fortress of stone. The girl awaited them, fruitlessly and modestly seeking to arrange her medium brown hair over her bosom. He who reached her first already had off his cape. Keeping his gaze only on the face of the unusually breasty young woman, he passed her the garment.

"Cover thyself, daughter."

"My thanks, sir knight," she said, without comment or smile for the fact that this man who called her "daughter" was no older than she.

She whipped the scarlet cape about herself in a swift act that imparted much movement to her large bare breasts. Of course it covered her only to the hips, and much bare pale leg was left shockingly visible. Too, as her mount moved shyly amid theirs to ascend the long hill at a trot, the cape furled back to reveal the constant snowy joggle of those melons. She seemed not to notice and did not try to hold it together. No Hospitaller looked, or seemed to.

They were many more minutes returning to the fortress than they had been in descending.

"God help us all," Aimar murmured. "Rigord—do you go at once to my chamber and fetch out a good cloak for her from the gifts of Richard the King—a *long* cloak, mind! See that it envelops her within a second after she dismounts!" Mentally the Master added, *God and Saint John His holy apostle preserve Brother Rigord and us all from the temptation of a woman fair as the clouds and with the udders of a nursing nanny-goat!*

Though not so much adangle, those big firm masses, Aimar the Unsmiling thought on, and on the instant assigned himself an hour's prayer on his knees this night, as penance for the thought.

She was swathed in a great mantle of royal blue when the Master came to interview her, in his robe and cloak of dull black unrelieved save by the rosary that swung its heavy cross at his sword-side, nearly to the knee. Her cloak, a gift of Richard of the English to the Hospitallers of d'Entremont, was so long as to obscure even her feet. Even so, he was sure that they were small, with delicate little toes like pale chick-peas. She looked pale, harried, and bedraggled, and her hair was sadly mussed. There were no combs in the fortress; God was no admirer of vanity. She was also so beautiful and sensuous, somehow *animal* sensuous, that he swallowed. Outsized blessing of an overly kind God, her glorious bust thrust out the cloak so that the fabric of it shone.

Shameless, he thought, and yet knew that there was nothing she could do about it; the Good God had blessed her with a figure beyond most women's; a figure to make many women resemble boys. Only nuns strapped down their bubs.

He tried not to look at the twin bulge of her nipples.

She rose at once when he entered, and he noted that she was unsteady on her feet.

"Oh my good lord, I am so grateful! I fled and I fled, and they . . . they . . ." She broke off her weak-voiced expression of gratitude, gazing so sweetly and beautifully at him from absolutely beautiful, sensuous eyes. "I am . . . I am the Lady L—" The poor thing broke off again, looking positively limp. "Poor girl that I am, I do thank thee my lord . . . for . . ."

Then her eyes rolled loosely and she pitched forward in a faint.

Taken by surprise, he nevertheless moved swiftly to catch her ere she could fall to the floor. He succeeded, and in one of his hands, all accidentally, was a firm and yet soft weight, smooth as a baby's bottom and large as her own head. It was her left breast. It seemed to burn his right hand, and in that moment Master Aimar was on his way to being lost.

As he moved her to a low couch or *divan* taken from the enemy, he was thinking of her words. "The Lady . . ." This was no camp follower, then, but a woman of rank. A lady. Nor did he see the opening of one of her eyes, and the way it rolled up to peer surreptitiously at him. He did not observe the little twitch at the edge of her lovely mouth, either; the faintest hint of a smug smile.

When he had caught her as she fell, her arms had naturally swung loosely down on either side of his robed legs. Now, when he lowered her to the cot, those arms remained in place and somehow her hands clutched, clung to him just at the waist. The poor demoiselle had escaped the godless Saracen, he thought, and been chased, terrified by them, and now clung to her savior even in the unconsciousness of her swoon. The thought was fleeting because he had other matters to occupy his mind: as he stretched her on the cot, her arms somehow pulled him down with her. He managed to catch himself with his knees on the floor beside her. The prostrate girl sighed, eyebrows sweetly arched as if in the serenity of sleep, and yet her hands clung.

He furthered himself on the road to perdition by not disentangling her cloying arms and rising at once, by not calling in others or at least another. His hand was helpless not to toy with that which had fallen so softly and warmly into it. Not since he was fourteen had he . . .

In her sleep, the dear maid surged that lovely mound into his hand. "Uh," she murmured, lips parting only slightly. "Oh, ummm . . . oh my darlinnng . . ."

Long used only for elimination, his penis behaved as if it had a mind of its own. It took on the hardness of a quarterstaff within his robe. It pressed against her. She was warm, it was hot; Aimar was hot all over and yet little shivers ran through him. He wanted to move, not from her but against her. Yet he dared not move at all, for to do so would have the effect of loosing the taught string of a bow, and he knew he would spurt his essence within his robe, against his leg, which was against her thigh . . .

It was she who moved, in her unconsciousness of course, sighing and writhing a little. He groaned as it happened, that which he had longed for and yet feared and sought to avoid. While he was moaning in orgasm, she decided that this was the best time to wake, and so she opened her eyes.

Looking almost sleepily up at him from beneath shuttering lids, she showed him a small smile. And one hand tightened on him, while the other moved . . .

"Oh you darling man," she murmured in a soft, lovely voice. "Here, let me . . ."

He groaned again, shuddering helplessly in pleasure and yet in some horror, as her hand slid onto his still twitching organ. She clasped it, stroked it, caressed that organ of wickedness he had so long denied. So long that in less than a minute it was again high and hard and athrob, and she moved this way and that, tugging at him and at his robe, and easily tucked his fierce new erection into herself.

"Ah!" she gasped, and threw back her head. "Ah, ah darling man . . . oh, I need your solace so, your tenderness . . . those filthy Saracen! I only just escaped—you have not

13

even—uh!—yes, yes move, move on me and in me! You have not even seen the stripe on my back, have you! Oh, oh my God, do, do that, oh yes . . . oh, oh! But how shameless I am in my need of being comforted—you do not even know my name, my lord Aimar. I am the lady Luisa à Vilmandeux, and you have saved me, saved me from a horrible fate! Uh, uh—ahhh . . ."

Thus did Lady Luisa de Vermandois come to the invincible castle, and conquer its unsmiling and invincible master.

"*I love the mêlée of shields with blue and vermilion tints, flags and pennons of different colors, tents and rich pavilions spread over the plain, the breaking of lances, the riddling of shields, the splitting of gleaming helmets, and the giving and taking of blows.*"

—BERTRAN DE BORN

ONE

The Saver of Kings

"Way! Make way there, for Guy Kingsaver of Messaria!"

Desperately trying to urge more speed out of the horse that had belonged to Conrad of Montferrat, Guy of Messaria galloped down Tyre's sloping street after the fleeing gray-cloaked rider. He saw her black steed bear down on a child, heard its shrill scream of terror. The pitiful sound was cut off in mid-cry. The small form was slammed against a building to rebound and tumble in the street, a red ruin.

In seeking to guide his own horse around that pitiful form, the Crusader lost precious seconds in his pursuit of a traitor and spy for Saladin. His mount's foot slipped and Guy leaned the other way as the animal reeled, its hoof slicked with the blood of a child run down for no reason save that its rider was heedless of all life save her own.

Both steeds raised a great clatter on the pave with iron-shod hooves, and Guy continued his yelling, so that other potential victims got themselves out of the way. The nighted street declined steadily and almost sharply, and Guy heard clearly now the sound of waves slapping shore. His quarry raced down to the shore, and turned along it. Following at the gallop, he saw her destination, and could barely believe his eyes. There lay the sea, flashing like dull gems in the light of stars and a pale moon. Sparkling wavelets lapped at . . . an enemy ship! Bobbing out there at anchor, sail only partially furled. Waiting. Off the very coast of Tyre!

Where was the city watch of this damned city of over-powerful chamberlains and arrogant guardsmen?

God's Own Blood; the ship had even put men ashore! Nor were they disguised; he saw their minarets of helmets, surmounted by pointed spires. Soldiers of the paynim— Turks!

Even as he saw them, he whipped his cloak about his left arm. Bending low, long sword trailing and ready, he clapped heels to horse and charged them: across the rock-strewn sands directly at the little band of armed Saracen who stood ready to deal death in the darkness.

Whether they wanted to face the charge of a mailed and mounted man or no, they must; the gray-cloaked arm of their lord Saladin's Christian spy pointed back at her pursuer. The big iron hooves of his mount hurled up clots of wet sand as, bending low with its mane stinging his face, Guy Kingsaver hurtled at them as if launched from a mangonel. The foremost Turk tried to back, stepped on the foot of the man behind him, and received the full impact of a rushing horse trained for war; trained to turn aside for nothing save the signals of its rider. The man was actually hurled through the air to smash down six paces away. Silvery steel flashed bright and another shrieked at the loss of his sword-hand to Guy's rushing blade. Then Conrad's horse was through them, snorting in excitement, turning in response to the signal of its rider's clamping legs.

He pounded around to charge again, so obviously a war-trained destrier who loved this grim work that Guy silently thanked Conrad, for he loved the animal and counted him comrade and friend.

The fleeing spy who was his object was already dismounting in a rush, aided by the dark hands of a waiting Turk. At the same time she was clamorously telling of her saddlebag and the casket it contained. Another Saracen whipped off the bag, grunting, but she greedily seized it from him and bore it as if it were no heavier than a goose-down pillow. In a swirl of pearl-gray mantle, she swung with it to the longboat awaiting her just at the surf's edge. Three men manned its oars, three dark men with pointed black beards. Behind her, Guy was charging anew, fully intending to burst through the soldiery and trample boat, oarsmen, spy and all.

The soldiers intervened, and amid a scraping ring of sharp steel on link-chain legging, Guy felt a blow and pain in his right leg. Only the mail had kept him from losing that leg to the well-swung symitar, and he chopped viciously at its wielder so that the Saracen moaned and let go his sword while his hands leaped to his slashed and spurting face. Other men struck, and at sea's edge their quarry kicked his right foot free of its stirrup and used the other to hurl himself into the air, over his horse's neck, over the shouting soldiery of Islam.

The oarsmen stared with enormous eyes and one was so reckless as to start to stand in the boat. Yet he had not even time to leap into the water. Like a missile hurled by a siege engine, the flying apparition of scintillant mail and gleaming sword came rushing through the air. The Crusader strove to fold his legs as he came down in the boat feet-first; two hundred pounds of tall farm-bred youth in eighty pounds of armor and harness, plummeting like a boulder. With a rending crash, the boat capsized amid the yells of two oarsmen and their gray-cloaked passenger. The third rower had taken the point of the human missile's sword.

Heavy laden, the saddlebag went straight to the bottom of four feet of water.

Attacker and his quarry spluttered, floundering in the surf. Only two oarsmen came up. The blood of the third darkened the water, along with swirling mud. The Crusader's steel carapace had become a hindrance now and his right thigh was aflame within that armor. He faced two angry men who wielded long oars of seasoned wood. From the corner of his eye he saw their passenger wading ashore amid curses and staggers in her water-heavy woolen mantle. In a rage, Guy slashed at one man and jellied the face of the other with a mailed fist. It was the hated Saladin's spy he wanted, not these two, and he slogged after her. Water spurted forth from the interstices of his chain-mail. Far up the strand at the mouth of the street down which two horses had galloped so madly, torches were bobbing now, bright yellow above a group of men. Seeing those along the beach and the enemy carrack beyond, the Tyrians raised excited outcries and came arunning.

And Guy Kingsaver waded back to shore.

A snarling man with a split black beard and a helmet adorned with a heron feather met the Crusader as he waded in, and his curved sword swept back and streaked out at him. The huge man in steel ducked low, his thigh practically screaming as he dropped into a crouch. His own sword-stroke destroyed the Turk's knee. Another scream split the night.

Just beyond, the bedraggled woman in the gray cloak was dancing up and down on the wet sand, waving both hands. *"Get That Damned Boat* UP!"

Guy made an error, then: he glanced at her. His foot came squelchingly down on wet sand as he reached the strand. He staggered a little, jerking his glance back from the yelling woman—and looked at the Turk who stood no more than six feet away. It was not at his face that Guy of Messaria stared, but at the steel shaft of the Muslim's leveled crossbow.

Desperately the Crusader hurled himself aside. He felt the heavy blow and flash of fire in his side at the same time as he heard the metallic *thung* of the crossbow's discharge. Guy toppled backward into the water and seemed to fall and fall through wet blackness that whelmed both his bleeding body and his mind.

After that came five days and six nights of delirium.

Today the hero Guy of Messaria had risen and walked, for the first time in seventeen days.

Sixteen days and nights had passed since he had been wounded in his attempt—and failure—to save the life of a future king of Jerusalem...

Seventeen days and nights had passed since he had saved the life of the future king of Jerusalem...

Three days had passed since the convalescing Crusader in his sickbed had been visited by his grateful friends, the King and Queen of Jerusalem...

His side hurt no longer and itched only now and then. Almost that steel arrow had missed; it passed through flesh only, without damage either to muscle or internal organs. Yet he had collapsed in sea-water along the city's coast, and infection had set in. He might have died. Perhaps his body tried to die; certainly he sank low. The indomitable will driving that body, however, resisted the skeletal hand of Lord Death. The Crusader had refused to succumb. Today he rose, and walked, and felt only an occasional twinge of pain that was not worth acknowledging or mentioning.

In Jaffa seventeen days past he had saved Henry, Count of Champagne and cousin of both the King of the French and of the English, from an assassin's blade. Immediately Guy had ridden the forty miles to Tyre in one long and grueling day. The startling feat exhausted two horses, but their rider could not afford to be exhausted. He had ridden so hard to thwart the plot to murder the man who was about to receive Jerusalem's crown: Conrad, Protector of Tyre.

Guy found that unworthy adventurer not at home; Conrad had gone to visit his mistress.

The Crusader caught up to the man seconds too late to save him from the assassin's steel. Conrad fell dead in Tyre's street. At least Guy swiftly did death on the murderer. He had almost exacted vengeance, too, on the treacherous instigator of that murder. Almost. Not quite. He did chase her to the sea, and into the sea. She was a spy and a plotter, and her comrades awaited her there with a swift ship. Guy chopped his way through those Saracens...

Until he met the Saracen crossbow. He heard its twang at short range, felt the blow in the side, and the pain, and after that he knew only delirium. He had not awakened for six days. During that time he had visited the shores of the domain of Lord Death, and spat thereon, and had come back.

The Crusader lived.

And now...

Both dead Conrad and now handsome Count Henry/King Henry had wed the heir to the throne of Jerusalem, Isabella of the red hair and impatient loins. They were her second and third husbands, poor girl.

Poor husbands!

Neither knew that the son of Peter, peasant of Messaria on Cyprus, had enjoyed her loving and her body, had cruised on a pleasure voyage up her wet loins before either of those husbands. Yet Guy of Messaria did not love her, and presumed that she did not love him. They had but pleasured each other, youthful queen and more youthful Crusader, for she was a more than sensuous woman.

With the aid of her lady-in-waiting, Blanche, Isabella had tricked him in the dark to gain him in bed, to accomplish the enjoyment of his body. He and she did not love and had not loved; they had but fucked. For it was fucking that Isabella of Jerusalem needed, as well as the warmth and security of love. But she was a queen.

During all these seventeen days Guy's physician had been the queen's own, while his nurse had been her lady and frequent companion, the blond Frenchwoman named Lady Blanche.

With Guy Kingsaver, Blanche was no lady. Thanks be to God!

"Wed for the third time," Guy said incredulously, frowning as he sat propped up in his hated bed, "and her second husband dead but a few days! God's blood! How old is my lady Isabella, Blanche?"

"One-and-twenty."

"God," he muttered, "poor lady. She be only a crown— with a convenient womb attached!"

"I thank God," Blanche said, very earnestly, "that I was not born of royal parents."

"And I!"

For that was the problem. Isabella was heir to the Christian kingdom of Syria; the Holy Land. Never mind that Jerusalem was in Saracen hands and had been now for many years; her title was Queen of Jerusalem. And she must have a man, a husband, a strong king. Unwed, she became a tool and a pawn—a valuable pawn.

"I am daughter of the king of all this land," Isabella had said in sadness, "when there *was* a kingdom. Now . . . now Tyre is all I have."

About wedding Conrad she had little say. The Frankish barons had surprised Richard by choosing Conrad over a worthier, though older and less militarily accomplished, candidate. Isabella accepted that choice, for Conrad had at least earned the title Protector of Tyre.

But then he was dead, dead in the night, and all unknowing did the handsome Henry, foremost lord of France after the king, come riding.

He entered Tyre in much surprise, for people were hailing him as King! Through none of his doing, they saw and they chose, and in short order Isabella—for the sake of the kingdom, offered him her hand. Even more perplexed, Henry wrote to the true leader of Frankdom here in the Holy Land:

23

Richard, Duke of Normandy, Aquitaine and Poitou and King of the English.

King Richard urged him to accept crown and Isabella at once (the crown first, if possible, so that his claim to the throne would be his own, rather than as her husband), and then "tell Henry to come back to the host and bring with him the French, quickly as he can, for I want to go and take Darum—if the Turks dare wait for me there!"

And so on the fifth day of May in this year 1192, only eight days after Conrad's slaying, Isabella wed for the third time. Thus did Jerusalem gain a king, and thus did the wealthy and handsome bachelor Henry gain a crown . . . to the mutual delight of his cousins, Richard and Philip King of France.

Next day King Henry and Queen Isabella visited the sickroom of Guy of Messaria, son of Peter the peasant, to thank him. And to offer knighthood. And once again Guy sighed and said that he would wait to become Sir Guy at the hands of the Lion-heart.

Now three more days had passed, with the Crusader chafing that he could not join Richard and the army at Darum. Despite his walking about and proclaiming that he was fine and should be dressed and in a saddle, Blanche and the queen's physician, Ruzzik, persuaded him to resume his bed. Ruzzik of Seleucia extracted his big patient's promise that he would remain there for at least another two days.

"But they are saying that it was the Old Man of the Mountain who ordered Conrad's death, Guy, and sent his sect of assassins to accomplish it," Blanche said, once Ruzzik had rustled away in his fine robe, a gift of Isabella.

Guy gave her a look. "Aye, and milord the Bishop of Beauvais is saying that was my lord Richard who ordered Conrad's murder, so that Richard would be unquestioned ruler here . . . save for Saladin. As if my lord of the lion's heart could be so small—as small as Bishop Philip! God does not mind that His churchmen lie and plot; God does not care! Well, both stories are wrong, Blanche. One a lie, the other an error, that's all. It was Saladin who ordered Conrad slain. Probably because he thought that with Conrad dead, old Lusignan would be king, and an easy foeman. Was Saladin who sent that so-clever and ever-treacherous witch—his *Christian* agent—to Tyre, to snuggle up to Conrad! Was she who led him out for a ride that night, and into the hands of waiting assassins. Her reward for betraying a fellow Christian, *again,* was that casket of jewels I made her drop in the surf, the filthy bitch!"

"Thank the Good God for that," Blanche said excitedly, and her eyes shone like those very jewels from the coffers of Saladin the Turk. "A casket of fine gemmy gauds one-fourth of which *King* Henry has granted to you, Guy! Why, 'tis wealth!"

The Crusader's big shoulders rose in a slow sigh. He looked neither excited nor happy. When he turned his head to stare at her, his eyes were so frightening that Blanche blinked and swallowed. It had been her good fortune to know the fierce lover, not the darker, fierce warrior that was Guy Kingsaver, the Human Crossbow. She was even grateful to this spy they discussed, for many months ago that queen of treachery had taught the arts of love to a peasant's son on Cyprus Isle. Blanche and Isabella had cause to know that she had taught well. He was more accomplished in the couching than most men, including older knights and lords born to wealth and grace and supposedly tutorage in the arts of love. A woman had taught him the way to make love to a woman.

"Put the entire box of bright baubles into these two hands," he said in a low ugly voice intense with passion, "and gladly would I exchange it for the throat of that foul creature!" Holding up those hands, he clutched an imaginary neck in

25

the air, and twisted so that the veins and muscle stood out all up his powerful arms.

Blanche de Fontaines shivered and swallowed hard.

"Oh, my love," she said low, and leaned in to kiss his shoulder. That told her he was overwrought; not only was his muscular shoulder tense, he hardly so much as glanced down her yellow bodice into her cleavage. Yet she liked passion in him of any kind, and so she goaded him a little . . .

"Guy? This traitor—tell me of her. How came you to know her?"

"Seems to me that I have. She was on Cyprus. She is older, though youthful in appearance, damn her! Was she who sought me out, and who taught me much in the lists of love. When we had shipped over to these coasts and were camped before Acre and its accursed tower, though, she found a noble knight who would keep her. She was scornful of me then, and insulting. Methinks I have grown ten years during this year of war—I am only a farmer's son, Blanche, who happened to be in the hayloft one night and saved a tall red-haired man from an assassin. Only afterward did he tell me his name—"

"Richard, King!"

"Aye. Well . . . many died before Acre, and too many not from steel or flung stones and boulders. There I met my first real love, Rosamonde. My love, Blanche, not just my bed-partner as Luisa had been. Rosamonde's lady died of the fever that ravaged us all, and then . . . then Rosamonde died. For no reason, as there was no reason for her to be there." Guy paused and swallowed, staring at nothing. Again he thought it: *God does not care.*

"So too did Luisa's new conquest die. She sought even to come back to me, then. I would have none of the whore. King Richard took her into his pavilion; he too was laid low by the fever and a disease I will not describe, and yet he needed and deserved a woman. Oh she is attractive

26

enough, Blanche, and seductive, and better than good in bed. Soon . . . in addition to the sickness that smote us and that damned tower that would not fall, we were assailed by another horror. The King sent out small parties of men in quest of food for men and animals, and they continued to be waylaid and massacred. We could not discover why—it was as if Saladin knew of our plans."

"Oh," Blanche murmured, her face showing horror as the light of understanding came into her eyes. "Oh, oh no."

"Oh aye! When next I saw and heard Luisa, was in the dark of night, lurking among the rocks down by the shore. With her was a Turkish lord. Just outside our very camp! I heard her tell him of the little body of men the King was sending out next day, and knew why and how Saladin knew of our plans! Hard as it was to believe, she was a traitor. Worse, she was Saladin's spy—in the very tent of the Lion-heart! Just then, however, she was in the arms of that Turk." He looked at Blanche with dour eyes. "Fucking. With her cunt she won me, and that French knight, and now this Turk! Had her cap set on Saladin, I doubt not, and mayhap the Pope himself!"

"From what you say, she might well succeed—His Holiness had better see to himself, should ever this Luisa person reach Rome!"

He glared at her with those flat, staring eyes. "I cannot joke about *her*, Blanche. And if God grants it within my power, I shall see to it that she never reaches Rome—or anywhere else save the gates of Hell, her natural home!"

"I'm sorry, my love."

He squeezed her hand. "So am I, Blanche. Was you stayed with me all the while I did babble and rave; you nursed me and cleaned me . . . you probably saved my life, and never never should I be harsh with you, woman!"

She returned the pressure to the hand that swallowed hers

and with the smallest of smiles said, "Well, only a little harsh...physically..."

Still he was not able to smile, or denied himself the pleasure.

"You heard her betraying us all, and witnessed their couching," she prompted. "Then what did you do, my love?"

"Couching!" His voice scorned the phrase and he corrected her: "They fucked, there on the rocks above the surf! I waited. They finished. He shot his infidel seed up her Christian belly! All hooded, she skulked back into our encampment like the traitorous thief she is. He mounted to hurry and tell Saladin all.

"How that lord of Islam laughed and sneered, when he saw me facing him, without armor and afoot! I killed him. Next day, once I had told milord Richard and he had summoned her there, I showed her the head of her Saracen lover."

Blanche trembled, and again her eyes had gone all bright. "Mother of God, what a man you are, Guy of Cyprus! She must have gone to pieces, then—certainly I should do!"

"Believe me she is not you, gentle Blanche. But aye, she could lie no longer. King Richard had her punished, then ...but I shall not recount that for your tender ears, *Lady* Blanche! Her punishment was terrible."

She leaned close. Breathlessly she said, "Tell me!"

He looked at her. He understood, at least to a degree. He stilled his sigh. She was excited by all this, he realized. Excited, and thrilled, as a passionate and sensuous woman. Deliberately he told her in succinct, harsh terms the treatment which Richard had ordered for the traitor who had caused the deaths of so many of his men.

"He had her bound, all doubled up into a package, bare arse upturned in about as obscene a picture as ever one might hope to see. I cannot remember how many men-at-arms and horse-handlers lunged into her, fore and aft, or how many times. Did she take a hundred spends up her foul cess-holes, or two hundred? I know not. Those were sturdy men, and horny. They were a long time ramming and cramming into her, and my king and I watched it all without the faintest feeling of sympathy for the devil's handmaiden they used so. At last they had done, but the king was not through with his vengeance for his dead men. Both her well-used fissures were stuffed with earth and sand. Semen and her blood made it mud. Finally, milord Richard had her sewn up, here."

Guy paused to pat his blond nurse in the nook between the tops of her thighs, and she twitched. Then a great shudder ran through her and her eyes rolled. She placed a hand on that same pale-furred bulge beneath her skirt, and pressed hard, digging her fingers into a cloven mound gone all itchy.

"Ah, God," she murmured, seeming to sag. Yet her hand squeezed his arm with a strength he felt, along with the heat of her palm.

"Having as he thought ruined her forever and for all men, destroyed her, Richard the king had her borne out toward Saladin's camp on a galloping horse. There she was dumped, naked and bound."

"God," she said again, her hand pressing her mount now as if guarding it. "But—she did not die, and Saladin did not kill her."

"No. She is a cat, Blanche, a prowling treacherous bosom-heavy brown-maned she-cat prowling the night, with as many lives as any cat. Months passed, and I came upon her fleeing from *Turks!* We 'rescued' the bitch, slew the Turks, and used her."

"Belike pleasing her in the process," Blanche observed.

"Mayhap, though we used her rough, I and my companion. It was rape. We sent her off onto a ship lying offshore— a whore-ship, you see. That, I thought me, was truly fitting for *Lady* Luisa!" Guy's face writhed, but did not quite smile.

29

For a time he only stared again at the wall opposite. Then, in a dreadsomely quiet voice, he went on. "Some German knight befriended her, poor fool. She killed him. She escaped, again. You know where next she appeared—doubtless after a visit to her master, Saladin. Here in Tyre, to bring about the murder of Conrad!"

Blanche sighed, rubbing his muscled arm. "And still again she escaped. To do what, next time? What a woman is this Lady Luisa de Vermandois!"

Suddenly she was on the bed with him, on him as he sat propped against the wall. Her mouth went to his throat, his nipple. Trembling, she felt his tense tremblor and mistook its cause and meaning. "Guy...Guy...oh sweetling, I want you! Take me, now!"

"God's blood, Blanche—I've been talking about *her* and I'm thinking about her still. We don't dare make love now. I'd hurt you, sure."

With a shudder and little giggle, she said, "Good then, rape me as if you had caught her," and she chewed his nipple to rouse him to the violence his story of treachery and violence had caused her to covet.

Abruptly he moved. Clamping her breasts so strongly in his hands that the firm flesh gave under its soft skin and she yelped, he yanked her across him. One hand leaped from bub to bottom in a resounding whack. Then he was dragging up her skirt, baring her pretty legs and that slapped rear-cheek. White, white was that skin, which had never felt the kiss of sunlight—or the bite of this land's sun, which its natives called the Enemy. She was panting hard and her eyes were wildly dilated. Still clamping one breast in a crushing grasp, he flopped her over, lying now on her back across his thighs.

"Insensitive nurse—it's resting I am supposed to be, and you bid me misuse this body and weary myself by raping you!"

30

She saw his brief smile, and then again a big hand leaped, this time to her head, which he pressed against his chest. Pale tresses flowed down onto his muscular belly as he sat, legs outstretched on the bed. Immediately and more than willingly, she began to gnaw at his sensitive nipple. Her hand glided up his side in a loving caress. His slid down her body in a harsh one, leaving her breast all tingly with the rush of blood back into compressed tissue. Over the smooth warmth of her belly that hand slid, and she surged it at him.

"Hooh!" She jerked wildly when he found her very wet and open vulva, and in an instant ensocketed his thumb in her, to the knuckle.

His penis grew rapidly into a cock while she nibbled and licked and caressed, and he agitated his thumb strongly in her, fucking her with it while she writhed and gasped and panted. Lewd juicy noises arose. The sound of their breathing grew loud in the chamber. She found the hot hard pole of his cock with her hand, and after a swift hard squeeze, played lovingly with it.

Her fingers glided tenderly, stroking the soft, soft skin of his organ, feeling its quivers and little twitches as it came even more adamantly erect. Her movements became erratic, as he continued the strong and rapid movements of his arm, his hand, his thumb; thumb-fucking her while his knuckles grated over the erect twig of her clitoris.

"Huh—hmmm . . . oh, oh, ohh lover . . . oh G-Guy . . . loverr-r . . ."

Then she was gasping, jerking without control—and he stopped. With a whimpering sound, she turned pleading eyes up to him.

"Bestride me, wench," he told the nearly tearful blonde.

"I—I'm so close . . ."

"Aren't you! Good, then. But that is enough of my little thumb—take the real thing, wench. You want that final trip over the edge—work for it! Fuck me! Ride, milady knight, ride your destrier!"

Whimpering little complaints, she rose onto her knees and bestrode him, holding his hard staff straight up between her descending thighs.

"Uh," he gasped, as the helmet-like head disappeared into her and felt big, big, rearranging her labia and inward tissues with relentless aggression.

Her eyes went wider and wider as she sank down onto him. More and more of the shaft vanished up her swimming cleft and her needy lower mouth swallowed it hungrily. It was nevertheless sternly expanded, forced ever larger to encompass the girth of his cock. Then her yellow dress, which he had never bothered to remove, fell down to obscure the joining of their bodies.

"Hoist that dress and hold it up on your shoulders to display yourself, milady wench! And ride, ride!"

"Hmp...mmm..." she breathed out, high-voiced, and squirmed around on him so as to make his thick erection work within her.

She hoisted her garment, right enough, but did not stop at her shoulders. She dragged it all the way off and tossed it from her while he happily watched the bob of her breasts, the surging of their hardened nipples against her shift. Next she caught up the hem of that thin garment and raised it, too. Stripping it off and shaking out her hair, she leaned forward with the shift in both hands, and pressed it over his head.

Fluidly naked, she rode him that way, her calves bulging braggily of their musculature as she jacked herself up and down his strong shaft. He remained behind and within the cloying muslin until he needed both breath and sight of her. Then, blindly reaching out, he found her breasts unerringly and thrust her back, to relieve his head and face of gauzy cloth.

32

His rider was jogging rapidly now, and gasping constantly while her blond hair flew. She managed a smile when their eyes met. Then she tossed away the undergarment and rode her destrier until she could not get her mouth closed and was too sweaty and weary to ride him more.

Heedless of a little stitch in his side, he seized her with both hands on each side, just under the ribcage, and easily bounced her up and down amid the sounds of gasps and moans and lubricious squishing. Bare buttocks, already damp with perspiration, slapped him with sharp sounds of fleshy impact. Her hair flew and her breasts bounced and her eyes rolled madly as if they might fly from their sockets.

Orgasm hit her so hard that she wept and jerked sharply with it before going absolutely limp.

Letting her flop onto her side and turning onto his, he gorged up her, barrage-fucking with strength and copious wet noises, cramming hard and high and whipping back to spear deep again, until he was shivering, gasping, and jerking against her while he groaned out his own climax.

"Well," she said a longish while later, smiling weakly, "I did say a little harsh, physically, didn't I? Oh, oh Mother of God I *loved* it! I love you, my sturdy steed!"

"Shh. Ruzzik bade me rest. Strange—I felt no weariness, then."

"All too often, surveys of the crusades . . . disregard Islamic commitment and faith . . . It will be shown that Muslims believed themselves to be fighting for the One God of the True Faith, no less than Christians."

—RONALD C. FINUCANE, *Soldiers of the Faith;*

1983

TWO

The Trouble With Chamberlains

Two days after the Feast of the Ascension, Guy Kingsaver requested audience with the King of Jerusalem.

He was surprised to learn that the husband of Queen Isabella had quietly stipulated that he wished to continue to be called only milord Count of Champagne. It was no surprise that milord Henry was worse than busy, having so recently taken wife and ascended the throne. Guy did not need to be told, and was told anyhow by the self-important chamberlain. He was aware that many things had to be seen to and done, and many letters dictated and written. He also knew that Richard had urgently requested that his newly royal cousin bring the French to join the main crusading force.

Still, though arrogance had not raised its head within Guy Kingsaver, he had reason to believe that he was special. That was true, he was told by the silk-encased chamberlain with the cold eyes under superciliously arched brows; not, however, special enough to be admitted today.

Not happy with that, the Crusader strove not to show it. True, would have been fun to pare off the emerald-robed chamberlain's paunch and stuff it down his gullet, but Guy forebore. He went away, and found somewhat to do to ease the tension.

His inspection of his armor discovered the fact that Blanche had already caused it to be cleansed and hung in a dry place, that no rust from sea-water might weaken any of its many,

many quadruply-linked and butted little circles of steel. He sharpened his sword and tested his strength against his wire-wrapped bow, which was as long as his height. Each arrow he inspected minutely before slipping it into the quiver that was a gift of Blanche and—secretly—Isabella; it was decorated with strands of their hair, mingling the red and the blond. Having received his share from the jewel-box intended as Luisa de Vermandois's reward for treachery, he reduced Blanche to tears by hanging the necklace of gold chain around her neck, so that the lion-head pendant emphasized her breasts by lying heavily between them. It seemed to glare forth, with its two fine emerald eyes.

"But Guy, I cannot—"

"You can and you have and you will. It was mine and I want it to be yours, Blanche. It is yours. And you will please keep the rest of the baubles safe for me. I cannot be carrying them about in the field! *And* look after the horses I do not need, now that my own Deukkak is here."

She was weeping. She said, "Horses?"

"Milord Henry has stated that Conrad's horse, which I bestrode . . . that night . . . is mine, with its saddle and trappings. The gelding is a good destrier, a war-horse, and the day may come when I need him. For some reason, Milord Henry chose also to present me with another steed, from his own stables—"

"For your part in saving him from murder nigh three weeks ago!" she burst out.

"Umm. I, uh, possess two others, which will be coming up from Jaffa with the Duke of Burgundy and his men."

"You do! I had no idea that you were amassing wealth, my love!"

Guy looked even more embarrassed. "Hardly. A few battle tokens. Do see to them, won't you?"

"Sweetling—you know I will, but why must you go?

Tarry here with me, and wait until Champagne and Burgundy leave, at least..."

"I am healed and hale and my place is with King Richard and my fellows. That I was to tell Count Henry today, but he was too occupied with matters of the kingdom to see me. My feeling is that I need not his permission, but do this anyhow. If he still cannot see me come morning, then morrow night I shall leave him a message, and be on my way."

She turned from him, looking rather frail of a sudden, her shoulders seeming to shrink within a gown of a green he thought too dark for her.

"I—I do not want you to go," she said, to the silken-tapestried wall.

Guy opened his mouth, closed it. Some questions were far better left unanswered, he knew, and no statement need be answered. Why pretend a noble heart, dissemble, and pretend that it was because she was the *Lady* Blanche, and he was not even so much as Sir Guy, much less a genuinely noble lord? Why mention Leila or other women? Why restate his desire to *go*, to be with the crusading host at Darum?

He wanted to go because he was Guy of Messaria, and he wanted to go, and do.

They dined alone together that night, and he was pleased that she had rather be alone with him in his "sick" room than to display herself and her new jewellery among the others of Tyre's courtiers. She wanted to suck him, and he was nothing loath. Then she wanted to play at rape, and he denied her that. God's blood, how was it that what women feared most was rape, and yet it was a game they wanted to play, along with gaining a measure or semblance of violence, of *possession*, from their lovers?

Guy loved women; he understood men and combat.

He slept on his left side, turning up the scarred right; she snuggled close behind him, spooned to his body so that he felt her silky pubic hair against his bare buttocks.

Next day, in bright blue tabard over pale green leggings and white bliaut or tunic, he was again before the chamberlain.

"It does appear that Milord Count will be busy all this day," the fellow told him.

Guy compressed his mouth and grated his teeth. He turned to walk away, then swung back.

"I have fought in battle against the Saracen with that man, and I have saved his life, and I have more than two gifts from his two hands. Now methinks I shall seat myself here on the floor and be very quiet while you transact your important business. And when Milord Henry emerges, I shall ask what might have happened had you told him I wished brief converse. Then shall we learn whether he has ceased to be my friend or whether you answer for him. What else can you do, my dear Master Letold, other than sit and be important?"

The chamberlain's face went quite red. "You cannot— you may *not* seat yourself on the floor here, fellow, no matter how many gifts you have of milord's hands, or how important you think you are!"

"Oh," Guy said, and seated himself on the tiled floor on the side of the door opposite the officious chamberlain's official table, which was Syrian, all ornately carven of fine sandalwood and some other wood the Cypriot did not recognize.

"You Cyprian upstart—Guard!"

"Sir!"

"Remove this man from the floor!"

The middle-aged pikeman started forward, stopped to stare. "Sir? That be Guy Kingsaver, he who saved the life of both Christian kings in this land!"

The chamberlain went redder. "Devil take you both! He is insolent and making a spectacle of himself in this corridor,

38

varlet, and you are to remove him."

"Remove me, Jacques," Guy said quietly. "I shall not fight. I admit to being a trifle heavy."

The guard looked from one man to the other. "Sir!" he said, looking directly at the chamberlain with a very earnest expression. "Something seems to have befallen my ears— I cannot hear you, sir!"

Starting to purple, the chamberlain stood. The big-linked gold chain on his chest shifted, glinted above the full-moon thrust of his belly.

"GUARD!" he bellowed.

The guard looked perplexed, and industriously smacked his ear. The chamberlain reached for the fellow's pike. The guard withdrew it hastily, also giving back a pace. Off-balanced, the chamberlain followed because he had to take steps to remain on his feet. Two more guardsmen in blued armor and plumed helmets came racing to the scene from two separate corridors, summoned by that second shout. Guy Kingsaver swallowed and chewed his lip. He had never intended to cause such trouble. Then the tall thick door beside him was jerked open, from within the audience chamber.

"Chamberlain! What is this noise?"

Three guards, the chamberlain, and Guy Kingsaver stared at the handsome man in the doorway, and Guy scrambled to his feet. The newcomer wore a scarlet singlet over a yellow bliaut, red hose and trunks of a gold hue. The singlet was broidered in gold with the arms of the county of Champagne. His brown hair tended to curl, though he wore it short-cropped to accommodate the knightly mail-coif. Not only did the Count of Champagne not wear purple robes or the crown of the Kingdom of Jerusalem, he had a sword bared in his hand, long and broad of blade.

"Guy? Did one of these varlets presume to knock you down?"

"No, my lord."

"My lord," the chamberlain began, "this recreant—"

Henry of Champagne interrupted: "*Which* recreant, Master Letold?"

"This . . . this . . ." The chamberlain indicated Guy with a wave of one nigh-white fat hand bedizened with five rings. "This—"

"Master Letold? You refer to the man who saved my life as a recreant? Are you feeling quite well? Could it be the sun, do you think? Or the opposite—too much time in the shade of this palace, peradventure? How long since you have seen good honest combat, so good for clearing the head? Are you challenging Guy Kingsaver? How would you meet him—bows, perhaps, at a thousand paces?" Sternly the count added to one of the guards, "Cease that giggling, man. It becomes you but ill. Guy: surely I can trust you. What befalls here, that such a clamor is raised as to disturb me to come sword in hand to defend life and realm?"

"Milord . . . please milord, I had really rather not—" Guy was suddenly finding it very difficult to look at the handsome king.

"What were you doing on the corridor floor, Guy Kingsaver of Messaria? Who stretched you there? By the Cross—who *could?*"

"Sire!"

Count Henry lifted one eyebrow as he looked at the speaker, the blue-clad and -armored guard who had affected the hearing problem. He was a Frenchman of perhaps five-and-thirty.

"S-Sire . . . may I speak?"

"Would be nice," Henry said, "did someone speak. Aye, man, do have a try."

"Sire, Sir Guy did come to ask audience with milord, sire, and from what he said else, milord K—Count, I knowed that he first made the request on yester day. Master Letold was neither pleasant nor *especially* unpleasant, sire. Merely his normal rude self, sire."

Letold tried a bluster and his sovereign lord raised a hand for silence. As it chanced to have in it the sword Count Henry had doubtless forgotten having drawn, Letold not only hushed but backed a pace. His beet-hued face had faded to red, but had begun to edge back toward purple.

"He started away, sire, then turned back to advise Master Letold that he had noted as I had that Master Letold had not asked milord Count whether milord was too occupied to speak to him—Sir Guy I mean—and that he was going to sit him here on the floor until milord Count emerged, and ask his boon with his own lips, sire."

"Hmm. Ah. I believe I heard you, guardsman. It is possible that your lord even understands you. Do understand that when your lord is ready to be called 'sire' like an old man, he will advise you so. Are you telling me that my friend and the savior of my life and of my royal cousin's life wished to speak with me, and the owner of this belly would not allow him to do, or even apprise me of his desire? Do I have the gist of it?"

"My *lord!*" Letold essayed, and received a glare from his lord that should have crisped his cheeks.

Guy Kingsaver wished that he were far, far away. At the edge of the world, perhaps, and about to drop off.

"Uh-aye, aye, milord, uh, that be—that be the gist of it," the guardsman said.

Henry gave Letold another look. "And then? And then what happened? Do be hurrying, man; we have important maps laid out inside and the ink may well be fading whiles you lick your lips."

"Sir Guy did seat himself and Master Letold did command me to remove him and I did question him, sire I mean milord King I mean Count, and he did repeat the command, and uh uh uh, sire, I uh uh I said that I could not hear him"—

the guard dropped his head to study the floor—"and he did reach out for my pike, sire, and I backed a pace and he did mis-step and nearly fell and then he bawled 'Guard' at me again and these two did come running, doubtless thinking we was beset by Saladin and Satan theirselfs, sire uh milord, and then..." The guard floundered and broke off, disconcerted by the count's sudden smile.

"Why, that is really quite good," Count Henry smiled. "You do hit your stride as you go along, eh? Saladin and Satan indeed! You may be a minstrel and not know it, my friend! Can you sing?"

Quite red, the guardsman said, "S-sire ... qu-quite uh bad, sire ..."

"Ah-hmmm ... and you, Letold. Can you sing?"

"My lord?"

"I merely wondered if you might possess some talent or other, *Master* Letold. Sentries: to your posts. Saladin and Satan are not coming this day." The count started to gesture, which resulted in a wave of his sword. "By Saint Denis," he murmured, and sheathed it in his cross-slung belt of gold-worked cloth. "Guard—what is your name, man, and it sorrows me that I have to ask."

"Jacques, my lord, Gervase's son, from Froimont, sire. Milord."

"Ah. Thank you, Jacques. A man in my position always likes to have loyal men to hand, loyal men with the power of speech. Master Letold: you will come inside, please. Guy: I fear me that you must wait a bit longer, my friend. Just a bit. We have pressing business within."

Guy inclined his head in a bow. "Thank you, my lord. I understand, my lord."

"Wonderful. A man in my position always likes to have people about who understand things. Anon, Guy Kingsaver. Letold: attend me." Count Henry swung and re-entered the chamber.

With an absolute murderous glance at Guy of Messaria, Master Letold followed his master into the audience chamber. A moment later Henry's voice came clear: "Shut the damned door, Letold—think you this be a barn?"

Trying hard to feel guilty and missing the mark, trying not to grin, Guy of Messaria looked at Jacques. Standing stiff as a post, eyes straight forward, Jacques winked.

Thinking it best to say nothing, Guy forebore. They waited. Indeed, they practically held their breaths, trying to hear words from the other side of that tall broad door with its big bands of polished brass. They heard nothing. Henry of Champagne was not known for bluster, or as a shouter. Guy Kingsaver could not help but speculate on whether sword-steel might shear through brass, and how the yellow metal might hold up to a stout ram. Perhaps he might mention that to the count...

On the other hand, set as it was in mid-corridor with a wall opposite, no ram of real length could be brought to bear, here, and properly swung. Hmm.

The door opened. Master Letold exited the audience room, obviously bereft of both the gold chain and one of his rings. He looked distinctly unwilling as he faced Guy squarely and delivered himself of the words Henry had doubtless ordered:

"Guy of Messaria, hero, saver of kings and friend of my lord the Count of Champagne, milady queen and my lord the count request that you attend them within."

Jacques Gervase's son grinned openly. Maintaining a perfectly straight face, Guy dipped his head in a nod of acknowledgment—a signally brief one—and paced toward the door. Letold betook himself out of the way with considerable alacrity. Guy passed within, half-turning to close the door lest he be accused of tending a barn—and noting that on the inside the door was banded with black iron, solid and thick.

Then he turned, and was as if frozen. He was in a chamber of genuinely huge proportions, columned, gleaming of parquet floor in red, and white, and white speckled with pink. The tall, peaked windows of Araby with their feathery grille-work he was accustomed to, and liked. They reminded him of Leila, every time, although he was not sure why. The walls were hung with breathtaking tapestries of eastern weave and swirlingly complicated scheme and design in many colors. Impressive and beautiful, very ornate. Guy did not like them.

Fully thirty feet away two steps ascended to a semicircular dais of pink-veined, shimmering white marble. Henry of Champagne was there, standing, but it was the seated Isabella whom Guy first saw. Red-haired, slim and looking slimmer in her wine-red gown broidered in a filigree of cloth-of-silver. She wore a slim chaplet, the Queen of the Kingdom of Jerusalem.

"Letold," the count said, even as he gestured for Guy to approach, "makes a superb secretary and a rotten chamberlain. It is a problem with chamberlains; they feel that it is *they* who have the power, and too that they should *protect* masters from being 'bothered.' Letold has just become secretary again. Now my queen and I are looking for a chamberlain, Guy Kingsaver. May we consider you for the post?"

"My lord is not serious, for I am only a fighting man. If my lord and lady will forgive my saying it—I would suggest someone human be chosen this time, who dislikes not other humans, lest he serve you ill. For myself, I could not handle the post and its duties and am sorry to have been the cause of Master Letold's losing it. But on behalf of others I will say that I am glad, for he served my lord and lady not well. I be only Guy, of Messaria on Cyprus, and I am healed. Now I wish only to be permitted to mount and ride to join milord King Richard in the field."

After a moment of silence during which the royal couple

stared at him, Henry said, "And . . . that is why you desired converse with us, my friend?"

"Our friend," Isabella added quietly.

"Aye."

"You came to ask permission to leave Tyre and us . . . and Lady Blanche."

"It seemed proper, my lord and lady."

"Hmmm. Meaning that you are bent on going, but deemed it proper to pretend to ask permission before departing." The corners of Henry's lips hinted at a smile, and so Guy did not deny it.

"Those words are my lord of Champagne's. The Lady Blanche and I have made our farewells, and I wish only to ride to join the king and the host. I am too long separated from my comrades. They may need me before the walls of Darum. I would have said this on yester day, my lord, and left this morning."

"But for Letold, yes."

"Now my hope is to depart this afternoon, with your leave."

"You do not consider me a comrade, Guy Kingsaver?"

Guy was uncomfortable and did not know what to say; he found the words. "My lord King and Count toys with me."

The count looked surprised, not abashed. "You are right, Guy Kingsaver. It was not well said. As to 'may be needed' at Darum—Guy Kingsaver is always needed, and welcome wherever he is! Yet you know that I will soon lead a goodly force to join my royal cousin. Would you not tarry here and accompany us?"

"My lord . . . you await the arrival of the Duke of Burgundy and his force?"

"Aye. We two and our men shall march together."

"By your leave, my lord, I would be on my way before-

45

times. Perhaps I might play the rôle of courier, and save someone else the ride?"

"What we are trying to do in our gratitude is keep you here with us, Guy," Queen Isabella said.

"And what he wishes is to away from us," her husband smiled. "Well, never let it be said that Champagne kept Cousin Ric's best from his side! However: this afternoon is impossible, my friend. You will indeed carry despatches to my royal cousin, with my thanks. They will be ready for you by dawn."

"Then I may depart at dawn, my lord and lady?" Guy said. The last two words he added diplomatically and in politeness, though it was obvious that Henry made the decisions here. *He probably knows by now that she'd be happier as courtesan than queen. Go'bless her and keep her from harm!*

"Aye. And you will dine with us this evening, and we will hand you those things we wish conveyed to the King of the English and his host."

"And . . . and if I may ask, with your pardon . . . my lord of Champagne will not be called king?"

"He will not," Henry said at once.

As he bowed, Guy saw that Isabella did not look happy. Well, doubtless her husband had his reasons for preferring to be called a count of France than king over what little Christians held of this land. *Peradventure to remind all of that rich French domain of his,* Guy thought as he departed the royal company.

He dined with them that night, among many others, and spent most of the rest of the night with a weepy Blanche. He departed Tyre just after dawn. With him went two others. Guy had preferred to travel alone and Henry had wanted to send more men with him; they had compromised on two, a young knight and his squire, with extra mounts and lances.

"Who can stem a furious stream and a frantic woman?"

—*The Koran*

"Women are of little wits and lack religion."

—MUHAMMAD, *the Prophet of God*

THREE

Lady Luisa!

On her sixth day in Castle d'Entremont, its single guest
spent several hours atop the high outer wall. She merely
walked about as if in deep thought, while her long white
veil fluttered constantly in the gentle—and hot—breeze. The
Hospitaller sentinels tried their best to pay her no attention,
for now and then the breeze plastered her gown to her and
it hurt a celibate man to look. They were aware of the rumors
that she had become mistress to their stern Master Aimar;
every man was. None dared mention it even obliquely. Some
were angry even at the hint of a suspicion. Who could think
such a thing of the grimly ascetic Aimar the Unsmiling?

As for Aimar, he had been doing a great, great deal of
praying of late. Ashamed even of its cause, he kept that
prayerfulness from his men.

He knew that he was doomed and damned, for how could
God forgive him his sin? No day had passed that he had
not thought lustfully of the Lady Luisa, and no night had
passed without his falling once more into the gates of Hell:
that is, between her thighs and into the gates of her slick-
walled cunt.

She had even persuaded him to bathe, and rewarded him
by licking his penis and its pendants. Next she had taken
it into her mouth in a way that transported him to the heavens
even while he knew he was falling into the fires of Hell.
Rather than attempt to be as a nun in this place of celibacy,
she had taken what she wanted from those garments left

here by the Lion-heart. To some of them she had taken sharp steel and thread, that they might better fit her superb feminine form.

The fugitive they had taken in was a constant source of temptation, and Aimar constantly vowed to resist, and prayed for the power to resist, and as constantly fell still again. He had even acceded to her suggestion that both of them might enjoy his *mis*using her, and to her suggestion that he secretly fetch a hammer into the chamber. Her body had swallowed its haft as accommodatingly as it did his own hammer-hard organ of sin. She assured him that it had been most exciting indeed, and had proceeded to delight him by proving her extreme arousal.

This day she had persuaded him to allow her to pace the high wall, and in gauzy white muslin and cambric, at that. The poor man had no idea why she wished to pace up there in the sun, where even the breeze was hot. While the sun of May had become vicious, the stone keep of d'Entremont held a great deal of coolth in its shading, thick-walled grasp. Within that haven, the black robes of the Order were no less comfortable than had they been snowy. Thus she had succeeded in overcoming his objections to her wearing thin white garments during her promenade; she stated her fear of being overwhelmed by the sun's rays if she wore black or indeed any dark, heat-absorbing hue.

And of course she was irresistible.

It did not occur to Aimar that she might have been sent from God's enemy Lucifer to test him, for he was too sharply smitten to think such of her. Totally inexperienced, it did not occur to him just how very, very experienced was the Lady Luisa de Vermandois—Luisa à Vilmandeux, as she had identified herself here.

Nor could it possibly occur to him that she was here for a purpose, and further that eyes other than his doughty sentinels' were watching the fortress, as they had been every day since the lady's arrival. How could it occur to anyone that this day those vigilant eyes had at last been rewarded?

For they saw the signal: white cloth fluttering from the high battlement of the Invincible Castle, and reports were made and preparations set forward.

That night Aimar and his mistress received a scare on two occasions, when a Hospitaller knocked at the Master's door to report movements beyond the walls. Both times Luisa was mouse-quiet and awaited in her lover's bed while he cloaked himself and went to look. When he returned the second time, again with news that it had been a false alarm, she pouted—while stroking him—and made complaint. Then she recommended that he tell his foolish men how they were ridiculously spooky this night to no cause, and that he needed his sleep: therefore they were not to bother him unless attack was visible and imminent—and even then to act only if and when he gave direct order.

Aimar naturally thought that such a directive was going a bit far, and told her so.

She persuaded him by whispering into his ear around her tongue while her soft hand manipulated his accursèd organ and the fingertips of her other hand plucked at his more sensitive left nipple. He succumbed. Again she concealed herself and was absolutely silent, while he called his aide to him and issued the order.

Thus assuring them of no further interruption, he returned to nursing like a child at her capacious breasts, while she did this and that with her fingers . . . Soon she was groaning and writhing beneath his frenetically humping body. Once again she took his seed in wild spurts and saw his look of guilt at his dreadful weakness and sin. As before, she covered herself and lay silent and still while he said his final prayers for the night and composed himself for sleep.

She lay with her eyes closed, surreptitiously pinching her

51

nipple to ensure that she did not fall asleep, until he was snoring.

Then, inch at a time, she edged away from him, and off the bed.

Silently she moved about the chamber, gathering her tools. He lay on his side as usual. Carefully she positioned the dagger just above his upturned left ear, and brought the hammer down atop its hilt with a strong stroke that imbedded the blade to the hilt.

Even as he jerked and blood gushed from his mouth, she used the hammer again, this time directly on his head. This time she heard his skull crack like the shell of an egg. His legs were still twitching when she, with the long, voluminous mantle of royal blue swathing her from hooded head to instep, hurried from that chamber of fornication and now murder.

With his own key she locked the door after her. Taking the key, she ghosted along the corridor on swift bare feet. Who could guess that it was not locked from within; who among the brothers of St. John would dare attempt forcible entry?

No one was abroad within the fortress. She opened the small door beside the great one in the inner curtain or wall, and left the keep to hurry like a shadow of death across the outer ward. She ascended to the wall, found the rope she had concealed, and made it fast round a merlon before spilling its length down that sheer stone wall. All this in the shadow of those stone merlons.

When the sentinel came pacing along, she was yards away, peering through a crenel into the night.

"M-my lady—what on earth do ye here at this hour?"

She kept herself enveloped in the cloak and put contrition into her face and voice. "Oh, Brother . . . twice this night the excitement of alarums roused me, and I could not get me back to sleep. I but came up in quest of a bit of the night air. I am sorry that I gave you a start, Sir Hospitaller. I am only a silly woman—mind me not."

Brother Fulk went on his way, trying to stay alert. Indeed he felt the fool and guilty as well, for twice already he had supposed he saw the glint of steel in the moonlight, and both times he had raised an alarm for naught. He sighed. He had no doubt that he would be chastised and assigned penitence by Master Aimar, come the morrow.

His punishment was to come much sooner than that. After the Master, he was the first victim of the plan of Saladin and Lady Luisa.

The first man up the stone outer curtain brought more ropes, and these of knotted silk for easier climbing. While Luisa made them fast and sent them snaking down for more scalers, the first invader hurried silently along the wall after the sentry. Brother Fulk heard a sound and turned, expecting to see the sleepless lady about whom he refused to believe those ridiculous and vicious rumors. He had not even time for an outcry before a rushing symitar chopped three-quarters of the way through his neck.

Moments later, stripped of his black night-cloak, the corpse of Brother Fulk plummeted to the ground below. It teemed with symitar-armed men with dark faces and hawkish noses, all with their helmets covered in gray cloth against a bright reflection in the moonlight. The previous little flashes had been deliberate, for the benefit of the sentinel that he might raise false alarms, as he had.

Soon the wall was alive with Saracens, and already the first several to scale it were on their way to the great gate of that outer curtain. More hurried down laddered walkways to race in silence across the outer ward to the small door in the inner curtain.

Thus the men of Saladin entered the keep of the invincible castle. Soon its big gate was open, the death-pit covered, and they were hurrying up the ladders to man the archery chambers that covered the area just within the gate. In that, they met two sentinels. Shouts arose and steel flashed. A Muslim fell wounded; two Christians died.

A barefoot Hospitaller went racing to the Master's door. Yet shout and pound as he might, he could gain no reply from Sir Aimar. At last a well-aimed arrow pinned that brother to the door, and he could but stand there while he died slowly of blood-loss. By that time men were everywhere and the air was alive with shouts and the steely clash and ring of arms.

Then the Turkish cavalry came galloping, every man snarling his hatred and lust for the letting of Frankish blood. No gate barred the way of their snorting horses. Brightly colored caparisons of silk fluttering amid the jingle of harness and the triumphant shouts of their riders, they pounded across the outer ward and through the inner gate. Hooves drummed on the planking over the death-trap just within that gate, and then they were clattering on the hard floor of the fortress called invincible.

They found a castle complement that had heard no alarm: the men of d'Entremont Castle were confused and only partially mobilized. Some of the brethren wore only their robes of jet cloth, and four had not even snatched up weapons. Dashing, bit-champing horses knocked them flying amid swirls of black robes or crunched them screaming underfoot. One wore a helmet, which saved him from the first whistling chop of a curved sword but not from the other one that sent his arm flying along the corridor where Saracen horses clattered and skidded on iron hooves. Other Hospitallers were armed and mailed, or partially. They were horse-soldiers, confused, trapped within walls, and without the horses that were to knights as the very earth underfoot was to other folk.

Desperately those monkish knights afoot sought to oppose mounted, slashing Turks on whom was no crippling confusion but only delight in conquest and the spillage of Christian blood.

Stone walls echoed the clattering stamp of horses mingled with the shouts of stabbing, slashing men and the ring and clash of their steel. Behind the Turkish cavalrymen, archers now came running into d'Entremont fortress, but they found no targets. Snarling disappointment, they began clambering up ladders, seeking enemies to feather with their shafts. About them the odor of fear and sweat and death arose to fill the air, and that worse stench as men evacuated at the moment of violent death. Hospitallers died and died and were trampled until the main corridor actually ran with the blood of goodly godly knights who never had a chance.

Soon Turks too were afoot, showing their white teeth like beasts as they dashed through the castle to make sure that no hated Hospitaller lived. Invasion led to battle, and battle swiftly became massacre.

Four armored monks managed to reach the final refuge, the keep deep within the castle. There they sought to barricade themselves. Within, they might have held out for weeks, with the keep's food supplies and store of weapons, and wreaked havoc on those men who came too close to slitted arrow-ports. A single valiant Saracen, however, engaged them just as they were about to close the door. Swords flashed silver and clashed ringingly. He wounded one man and sent another reeling, dizzied by a crashing ax-blow to his helm.

But they were four, and the yellow-plumed Turk took his death there, in the doorway.

While they sought to clear his body so that they might secure themselves within, a shouted command echoed and re-echoed along that bloody corridor. The teeth of the archers of Islam flashed in smiles; at last they had something to do! They went at their business with gusto, standing and kneeling in the space before d'Entremont keep. A great shower of arrows riddled the door, the corpse, and three of the Hospitallers within.

"Get the—door closed," one said, even with the arrow standing in his neck and moving with his words. "We will—fire the keep! They must not . . ." He had to pause and gasp, for blood ran from his mouth. "Must not take the castle!"

"And commit the sin of suicide, Brother Charles? Never! Say your prayers, brother, for we—"

That man broke off as coincidence betrayed him: a cross-bow quarrel caromed off the door, found a weak link in his mailcoat, and drove several inches into his back. He fell onto the others, and the battle for Castle d'Entremont was over.

Bearing the key to the locked door of the Master's chamber, Luisa de Vermandois was starting back across the grounds of the outer ward when drums rattled and a Turkish horn blared. She paused, gazing at the open outer gateway.

"Saladin," she murmured, for no ears but her own, and her face brightened in anticipation.

Through the lofty portal paced a fine black horse, tossing his head amid a jingle of the brass that gleamed on his harness of red leather. In the high-pommeled, high-cantled saddle rode a lean, proudly erect man. His faint smile was almost a sneer above a pointed beard that shone like oiled black silk. A tall white plume nodded above his helmet, which was finished in silver with gold scrollwork. The skirts and sleeves of his mailcoat had been finished with several rows of linked brass chain, so that the armor seemed broidered in gold. On his yellow shield a raging lion of the desert reared rampant and red, beneath the crescent moon of Islam. Of yellow silk were his shirt and his surcoat, and the latter was bordered in red-embroidered stars and crescents. Even so the most striking elements of his attire were his boots, which were tallish and white tooled with what was surely gold; and the white silken cloak that stretched behind him along his horse's back to its arched tail.

Very broad of shoulder this man with his face of a hunting hawk under his steel-curtained helm, he was lean of waist and long of arm. He could be called neither handsome nor ugly, but only striking and fierce, proud and arrogant. He stared straight before him with eyes black as the night pressing close about Castle d'Entremont.

Conscious of drama and triumph, the lord Emir Barak ibn-Yusuf al-Daula kept close rein, so that his horse must pace slowly and almost as if in a restrained dance.

Behind him came drummers and his retainers with their lion-and-crescent shields, and Luisa de Vermandois knew then that the Sultan was not coming. She sighed, at realization that his lordly cousin Barak was to take possession of the fortress in Saladin's name. That was disappointing, that she would not be praised and rewarded personally by the lord of lords himself.

Though they were grinning in pride and triumph, the victorious knights of Islam bowed before their lord. The only woman among them, the only non-Muslim left in this bloody place reeking of death, stood swathed in her long, long cloak of royal blue, and she did not bow.

The emir noticed, and reined in his high-strung steed, which snorted and pranced amid a tossing of its head.

"Ah, Lady Lovisa," Barak said, gazing down at her from his high saddle. "Already a courier is on his way to the sultan with news of your success and ours, in this night's work. Our lord Saladin will be pleased."

"He is not to come and inspect his new castle himself?"

"Nay; he has word that Malek Rik will most likely move on our Krak Ildris, and the sultan will lead the host there to dissuade the Franks. This fortress, Krak ... what is the Frankish word, Dontremawn?—he hath handed over to me, to repair and to hold."

"No repairs," Luisa de Vermandois said with pride, "will

be necessary! Some thorough cleaning up, of course."

"Very impressive," the lord Barak said, and vouchsafed his sultan's Frankish spy a brief nod of his plumed head in lieu of a bow. "Well done indeed! Well—wilt join me within the fortress, lady?"

Luisa met his cold narrow eyes, and put her head only a bit to one side. "Join you? You riding in, whilst I walk behind?"

He gazed serenely down at her from the back of his horse, eyebrows arched and face impassive, a man who wielded his power easily and casually, for he was strong, and the power was his, and he was sure of it. Suddenly Luisa wished that she had said nothing. He was going to answer, and other ears were listening while other dark, dark eyes watched, and she would only lose face because she had allowed herself to blurt those stupid words.

"Thou art an ally, Lovisa, and we trust and reward thee for a task well accomplished. Allah knows what gemmy rewards our mutual lord may load upon thee this time, once my messengers reach him with news of this night's work. You force me to remind thee, however, that I am his cousin and lord emir of Islam, and you remain, Lovisa the Frank, a woman."

He straightened in his tall cradling saddle then, and twitched the rein, and his mount paced prancingly across the turf and through the inner gateway.

No one laughed, or said aught. Yet Luisa would not look at any man, for she had no desire to catch one in a mocking look or some faintest of smiles. What could she do about it?

She held her head high and turned to walk barefoot into the keep she had gained him, and her cloak trailed the ground. If only she had said nothing! Now she had lost face, and in her hour of greatest triumph. And she might have lost more than that, she reflected bitterly. She was as

58

he said, a woman. Much meaning was implicit in that statement, although he had not quite said "only" a woman. That was implied. She was Luisa the Frank, a woman, alone, among men—and Muslim men at that. Any who thought that the status of the women of Christendom was low had only to read the commands of the prophet concerning them, and to take note of their state in al-Islam.

She did what she must and tried to put the best face on it by doing that which she could: She kept her head high and saw to it that she paced carefully and with dignity, rather than picking her way on bare soles.

The ugliness and the stench struck her the instant she passed within the conquered fortress. Her feet made wet noises so that she shuddered and the fine bright blue cloak dragged its hem in the blood of the men she had betrayed to the enemy of her people, her country, her god and her religion.

Lord Barak, she noted, did not dismount to sully his snowy boots. There would have to be a cleaning up, all right. This time no one had bothered to try to take prisoners; indeed, the attackers had decided not to. The Hospitallers were an old and hated enemy. Besides, who had they to ransom them, these men with their vow of poverty? They had served their god, and now they joined Him. Their blood trickled along the floor and pooled in shimmering blots of coagulation; dripped from steps and streaked the walls. The air was heavy with the stench of gore and cess ejected by men at the instant of death.

Krak d'Entremont had withstood attacks and sieges for over ninety years and gained the reputation of being unconquerable; of invincibility. Now it had fallen in a night— following a few nights of preparation, in bed. What the might of al-Islam could not accomplish, a woman had effected easily.

And now I have more to do, Luisa mused, as she looked

about her with distaste and listened to the orders of the new lord of Krak d'Entremont. Already she knew that she had a new mission. She had conquered the previous Master of the Castle, and now she must set about the conquest of his successor.

"O, when they cry 'Outrémer', dear God, help the pilgrim for whom I tremble, for the Saracens are bad."

—FROM A MINSTREL'S SONG

DURING THE CRUSADES

FOUR

Murder of the Innocent

This assignment was hard for Vulgrin of Montmirail. It was in fact a hell of a way for a man to begin his career as a knight. Yet it was Sir Vulgrin's task, and he did not despise it. It was his assignment from his liege-lord, the Count of Champagne.

Vulgrin had not even grown accustomed to hearing himself called "Sir," although he had dreamed of it often enough, during all those years of training while he was squire to Sir Jean. But a month ago Sir Jean had been killed, far from home here in Outrémer, the land of the Saracen. A week later Count Henry himself had presented his squire with the belt and the golden spurs of a *chevalier:* a knight of France. On the instant Vulgrin, Squire of the Body, became Sir Vulgrin.

Now Vulgrin rode under his own banner of green and blue and yellow with his own squire, on his first specific assignment from the count. And it was difficult. Vulgrin thought on it, as he rode beneath the broiling sun of the land variously called Syria, and Palestine, and the Holy Land, and simply Outrémer—"Beyond-the-Sea"—and even the Kingdom of Jerusalem.

One was born into the nobility, and one grew accustomed to the fact that one was a superior person. One *knew* it. There was no question. Holy Mother Church and all her prelates and (noble, lordly) bishops supported the fact that if one was of the knightly class, one was superior. Commoners, the base-born, deferred to the high-born. They got out of their way and obeyed their orders. Of course each noble deferred to his or her superiors, too; every man had superiors, for was even a king not subject to the Pope in Rome? Even when one was squire and subject to the demands and commands and indeed mere whims of the knight or lord to whom one was esquired, one was aware of one's superiority to those born to a different station and thus rôle in society. This was true whether a Vulgrin of Montmirail was a brat of three years or a squire of thirteen. (A year later, of course, he was officially a man and definitely on his way to knighthood and the respectful *Sieur:* "Sir.")

Vulgrin of Montmirail was nineteen years and five months of age. From his lance fluttered his own silken banner.

As squire, he had also been very aware that he was French, a Frank; that his was a lord of France. No matter that King Philip had returned to that far land of the Franks: he left Hugh, Duke of Burgundy as liege-lord of all the French in Palestine. Of course Richard of Normandy was a king and so the highest noble here after Philip's departure—except for Saladin, but who counted the godless Saracens? Duke Hugh was his own man, however, and Philip's, not Richard's.

Also as squire, Vulgrin had admired the big heroic islander called Kingsaver and the Human Crossbow. Only a dishonest bigot could fail to recognize the heroism and respect such a man—such a young man—and never mind his lowly birth.

Still, it made one to frown a little that Guy Kingsaver had been elevated to squire and had actually been offered knightly spurs. A peasantish farmer's son, of Cyprus! What might the world be coming to, when a peasant's son could be knight while a born and long-trained noble remained a squire?!

Nevertheless, Vulgrin of Montmirail admired and respected Guy of Messaria. Now he was not sure whether that fact made his assignment more difficult, or less. The point was that it was Guy—not *Sir* Guy!—who was Count Henry's messenger to King Richard, and the count had sent Vulgrin along as the big Cypriot's escort, rather than the other way around. Technically, Sir Vulgrin was at Guy's disposal and command, though the Cypriot had given no commands. Indeed, he was easy to like and thus a good and easy comrade. Better than Vulgrin's squire Radulph, who was quiet, unimaginative and perhaps not all that intelligent. And furthermore—surly.

As a matter of fact button-nosed Radulph was finding it a lot harder than Vulgrin, this business of being escort to and thus subject to a mere peasant's son and a foreigner besides, no matter how big and heroic he was or how many Turks he had slain and how many kings he had personally saved from death.

Thus the three rode from Tyre in the general direction of Darum: all armored and wearing the surcoat of crusaders; all well mounted and well armed. Yet their leader bore no lance, much less a pennon showing his noble armorial bearings or colors, for he was neither lord nor knight. He was not deferential, but he was polite. He was also an accommodating fellow. Although not overly given to chatter, he did talk, and amiably enough. Too, he made suggestions rather than stated mandates as orders. In the day and a half since their departure from Tyre, he had asked Vulgrin's opinion three several times, and once he had even asked Radulph's (something that Vulgrin would not have done).

And Radulph had continued surly.

I shall talk privily with the boy at first opportunity, Vulgrin thought. *He will either behave sensibly or I shall have to put embarrassment on him. Too bad for him if I asked him to draw that big wire-wrapped bow of the Human Crossbow! Methinks Radulph would not know that he need not be embarrassed—since so far no man has succeeded in drawing that incredible bow!*

When Vulgrin glanced over at him, Guy Kingsaver was squinting, looking upward. He lifted a mailed arm to point.

"D'Entremont," he said. "The Hospitallers' keep—see it there, just its topmost stones showing? In an hour or so we will be passing beneath it."

"Ah—ah yes, I see it now. Good eyes God has given you, Guy Kingsaver! See you its highest merlons, Radulph?—the castle that has never fallen."

Guy nodded. "Aye. And fall it must not, Sir Vulgrin, for this be the main supply road to our army from the sea. Without its presence there atop St. John's Hill, pilgrims and our supply trains would be in far more jeopardy than they already are—and so would we."

"These confounded 'pilgrims' have no business wandering about here anyhow," Radulph said sourly, "when the whole country is at war and they are merely targets for the Saracen and trouble for *us* to protect."

Guy Kingsaver expressed no opinion on that statement. Despite its callousness, it was absolutely true. Both camp-followers and well-meaning pilgrims were obstinately, stupidly confident that God would not allow aught to befall them, here in His own land. Such dolts only added to the responsibilities and worries and trials of the crusading army, as well as of the Hospitallers and Templars. The latter, residents, were chief guides and protectors for such "tourists."

"Well," Guy said quietly, "if that keep were in Saracen hands, we'd not dare keep to this road, much less expect to receive food and water and arms from our ships."

"God be thanked then that it is in the hands of the Hospitallers," Vulgrin said.

Guy smiled and glanced at him. "Amen. I like me not the thought of having to attempt to take such a fortress!"

"Oh I'll bet we could take it," Radulph said, and Vulgrin gave him a look. But Radulph was carefully not looking at him, just then.

Oh of course, Radulph the Overconfident because you know not enough, Vulgrin mused. *And I'm just sure that King Richard would place you in charge of the siege!*

They rode on, descending slowly to the valley at the foot of St. John's Hill.

It should not have happened. God should not have allowed it to happen! Everyone knew that it was safe to ride the narrow road in what to the Saracens was *Wadi l'-Azhara:* the Valley of Noon, and which westerners called St. John's Valley. The six of them had thought themselves completely safe here, and should have been. No one had told them that the impossible had taken place: that the great old Hospitaller fortress had been taken by the enemy. Even given that dread and fatal error, the Turks should not have attacked the way they did. Surely they could see that the party of six included three women, and that only two of the men were knights—Templars. Nevertheless, the first hint any of them had that they were in danger was the high-pitched squealing sound that announced a hailstorm of arrows rushing down at them.

Brother Roger and one of the Knights Templar were so unwise as to jerk their heads up to look; both took arrows in the face. Another drove through Sister Euphrosyna's veil and plunged into the back of her neck. She and the Templar were dead before they hit the ground. Poor Brother Roger lay with the arrow jutting from each of his cheeks, pinning his mouth while he drooled blood. No fewer than three arrows struck the other Templar's mount, and the man only just got clear as the beast fell. The girl Agathe had been standing in the cart, speaking to one of the Templars riding alongside. Arrows drove deep into her shoulder and into

67

her breast. After a brief beginning cry of agony, she lapsed into unconsciousness.

"Do not look up!" the unhorsed Templar shouted, but Sister Paulina had no intention of doing so.

She had felt the tug at her head without knowing that another arrow had passed completely through her veil, behind her; she was staring down at the shaft that was pinning her foot to the wooden floor of the cart and wondering why she felt no pain. She had no thought, then, of how incredible it was that the arrows had come from d'Entremont castle, or at least well up its hill.

Then more of God's enemies came galloping from some hiding place up the road. Silken pennons fluttered and flew brightly from their lances while the roadway smoked under the pounding hooves of their war-horses. Shouting out ululating Seljuk war-cries, they bore down on the tiny party of Christian idealists who had decided to bring cheer and nursing abilities to the army of the Crusade.

The Knight of the Temple met their charge with bared sword and an equally fierce cry. With a terrible *whump* sound of impact, the brave monk was knocked several feet by a huge gray horse so that his armor rattled against stone jutting up from the very earth. Brother Roger was also trampled in that first charge, so that he burst gorily open and knew no more agony. Sister Paulina saw Sister Euphrosyna trampled by steel-shod hooves, too, but she was surely already dead.

It all happened too fast for Sister Paulina to be certain of exactly what took place; she who had never seen so much as a drop of blood spilt in violence nor felt any true menace to her person. In that, she was ignorant as a child, and only a month in this land called Holy.

Amid blinding flashes of steel in the sunlight, the Knight Templar slew one of the Turks and girded his sword into the scale-mailed leg of another. Yet he too was wounded, and soon Turkish knights in yellow surcoats had made him their prisoner. A dark, ferocious-faced man with a nose like a vulture's beak bounded onto the cart to loom over Sister Paulina, who murmured her final prayers.

Yet he did not kill her, but spoke to her in the barbarous language she did not understand. He bent and with a jerk and a snarly laugh, drew forth the arrow that had miraculously passed between two of her toes. It had pinned her sandal to the cart without so much as scratching her. Just as miraculously, the young nun was the only member of the party who was unscathed. To her horror, the attackers slung the dead into the cart and bound the Templar on a horse.

Then, while Paulina tried to tend poor wounded and unconscious young Agathe, the cavalrymen of Islam took cart, horses, corpses and prisoners up the road to the Hospitaller fortress. Except that now it was a Saracen fortress. That she saw as soon as men in pointed helmets opened gate and toothy portcullis and she and her mounted captors paced and rattled in among grinning dark men of the desert, who babbled away in their godless tongue.

Soon she saw other things, and they were horror to a girl who was a virgin in mind as well as in body.

Twice-wounded Agathe was inspected and judged worthless to her captors. The Turk in the blue surcoat with the lion and crescent emblazoned on its chest pointed to her and barked a command. Paulina cried out when another whipped out his curved sword to plunge it into the girl's breast. He dragged it out dripping her gore only to drive it in again, and then again. A few words were addressed to the Knight of the Temple, traditional enemy of Islam. He answered proudly in Turkçe, his head high. Moments later that head of the Templar was bloodily separated from his body, and Sister Paulina's brain reeled within her swimming skull.

He who had given the death-commands cast his fierce gaze on her then, and she thought that she must die of terror before they could touch her. He thrust out his arm and pointing finger at her, and spoke. She knew he asked a question, but she recognized no word in his language.

"My Jesus mercy," she murmured, sinking to her knees and lowering her head far toward the earth.

If she had come here only to be beheaded out of hand, she had no desire to see the face and shining blade of her executioner. *Soon I shall join the blessed martyrs in Heaven*, she thought, and stared at the ground of the castle's outer ward, for all knew that those who were martyred in His name joined Him at once in blessed eternity. *I forgive my murderer, Holy God, hard as it is; I swear I do*.

She heard that same voice bark a command, and tensed, trying to steel herself while tears fell . . .

Sister Paulina, however, was neither a Knight of the Temple of Jerusalem nor was she wounded. Killing her out of hand was not the intention of her captor's leader.

Strong hands pulled her to her feet with ease and no respect for her person or her status as a holy woman dedicated to God. Bad as that was, it was far from all. Another hand just as callously stripped her veil and close-fitting headdress from her to reveal cropped hair. The Turks showed their awe and delight at its golden color even while they laughed and pointed at its shortness.

"Do not do this!" she cried. "I am the bride of Jesus—see? I wear His ring on my finger and am vowed—"

Then she could only shriek, for they tore from her the loose garments of black, and then of white, and the wrappings below, too. Her rosary rattled at her feet. And Sister Paulina was become only Paulina who had been Rosalba of Chalus in Aquitaine. A maid of eighteen, very white and lovely in her enforced nakedness.

She was well-favored and fair and knew it even though

70

she denied it in her mind and by the life she had chosen. For she had entered the convent only because she knew that the ugly old baron over her father's bit of land wanted her and intended to have her, so that she would never be dear Reynaud's bride, to work his little plot of land with him. She was fifteen, then. The lord of Chalus had even sent a woman to persuade her to leave the life of a *non-nuptae* she had chosen; when that failed, he sent men to trick her and bring her to him. They, too, failed. Though she had never been certain as to whether she indeed had a vocation to the holy life of celibacy and prayer, she proved an exemplary postulate and novitiate.

And all the while she heard of the new Crusade, and that even the lord of all Normandy and Aquitaine was to lead it: Duke Richard of the orange-red hair that was so like her own. And there behind the walls of the convent of St. Mathilde, she dreamed romantic thoughts of that far land, and of the shining knights of Christendom, and noble deeds. She could perform noble deeds too, she dreamed, though not with lance and sword, and armored only with the mantle of Christ.

Then came the final day and the ceremony in which she took the veil and the ring that wedded her to Him. Rosalba had learnt that Paulina, a very early martyr of Rome, had been young and fair-haired as well, and Rosalba was after all only an inexperienced and romantic girl of not-quite eighteen. With the veil and the ring, she took the name Sister Paulina.

Now she had borne that name for three months. At once she had begged to be allowed to travel to the Holy Land. She took the cross, too: pinned the scrap of cross-shaped white fabric to the shoulder of her black garment that none could deny her the right.

She had arrived here three weeks ago. And now . . .

Now she stood before hot-eyed, staring men as she had

71

never been seen even by members of her own sex: naked, stripped of all but the ring that bound her to her Savior. She could not even plead with them for they spoke not her tongue nor she theirs; nor could she attempt to cover her nakedness with her hands for the man behind her held her arms fast in the powerful grip of a warrior and slayer of men.

His head to one side as he gazed upon her, the commander of her captors rose smiling. Once again he pointed, and spoke words, and Rosalba/Paulina at last found succor from horror: she collapsed in a faint.

"You who speak her language will tell her what is expected of her, and what she is to do," the lord Emir Barak ibn-Yusuf al-Daula said, and he stared at Luisa dè Vermandois with eyes black as moonless night.

I had rather put a knife through her pointy little *titty and into her heart, or feed her poison,* she thought. For this damned whining virginal *girl* they had captured was a prize for the lord of Krak d'Entremont but none for his benefactress: the author of its fall. What of her plotting and her plans, when she was no longer the only woman available in Krak d'Entremont?

Damn! Damn her! Damn them!

But she showed nothing and said what she must: "As you wish, my lord Emir . . . but she is a nun, dedicated to the Christian God and even married to Him by the ring she wears. My lord Emir understands what this means; that she is sworn to a life of celibacy, with death preferable to forsaking that oath?"

"I hear you, Lovisa. And I tell you that if she dies before I have possessed that virginal white body, I shall hold you responsible. Does *my lady Lovisa* understand?"

You virgin-lusting son of a bitch-camel, I understand, all right, she thought, but held her face serene while she nodded.

"In that, Barak, surely I can succeed. As for persuading such a silly religious child even to pretend to enjoy the sexual gamboling which you and I love . . . as to that I can make no promises."

"How many well-guarded women were profaned . . . and pretty things put to the test, and virgins dishonoured and proud women deflowered . . ."

—IMAD AD-DIN, ARAB HISTORIAN

FIVE

Rape of the Innocent

He should never have asked the accursed Frankish woman's advice to begin with. Still, had it been a test he must consider that she had passed; her suggestions had been cruel ordeals she certainly would not care herself to endure! Nevertheless, it had all been a waste of time, albeit somewhat enlightening in more ways than one. Lady Lovisa was imaginative, at least. Perhaps a better word, Barak reflected, was *experienced*.

First she had her interview with the captive, and learned her name and origin, even a bit of her story. For that interview Luisa had been clothed as she had requested: in a Hospitaller's all-enveloping robe of black, the smallest one Barak's men had been able to find. That pointed up the girl's plight, Barak hoped, and would demean her the more—while giving her hope that she too might be clothed . . . if she were wise enough to cooperate.

She was not so wise. She told her "fellow captive" Luisa quite a bit, though nothing Barak deemed of military value. She absorbed the other woman's propaganda: that what Barak desired was not so bad at all, and was the key to good treatment, even clothing. All she need do was be a woman, a willing guest of Barak's couch, not merely one more rape victim. No, that the blonde would not do. Luisa pleaded, even managing to fetch up and shed a few tears as if for the plight of her fellow Frank. Paulina/Rosalba seemed not to judge her, but she continued to refuse. She was a different

75

person and a different sort of person.

"I shall call her Rosalba, then," Barak said afterward, while he and Luisa discussed her conversation with the girl, and Luisa's failure. "Her real name, and one that does not remind her of the stupid religious vocation she chose."

Luisa de Vermandois nodded, and her earrings swung and flashed. They were large loops of silver wire, in the style of the East. She had been more than happy to get out of the coarse robe of black and into a fine gown long ago left by the Lion-heart, Malek Rik. White and pale blue and dark blue, it fitted her very tightly to the hips, emphasizing her good waist and large bosom; Barak did not know that Luisa had altered the gown a bit, so that it displayed more of the naked curves of those big gourd-like globes. Below the hips it fell in full, graceful folds to brush the floor.

"Well," he went on, "she must be punished, and softened up. Then she shall do as I want her to do, just the same. Do you have a suggestion?"

"Two," Luisa said, and proceeded to suggest that the pale, pale body of her fellow Christian and Frank be tethered flat on a castle roof, tedded like leather to cure in the sun; and of course she mentioned the ancient remedies involving a whip, and the long ovals of Sister Paulina's very white backside.

The Turk shook his white-turbaned head. "The sun will only darken that lovely fair skin, and worse, in a very short time it will burn it so that she is sore and will peel as your kind does. I want no such ugliness! As to whipping her— I am also not interested in scarring those pretty hinder cheeks of hers!"

"One need not whip to scar, my lord Emir."

"No."

Seeing that he was set against a nice beating, Luisa shrugged—in a move calculated to draw his attention to the liquescent movement of her breasts. "She would be demoralized and horrified were her nose to be ringed," she suggested smoothly, still hoping to get the damned girl marked somehow so that she would be less attractive to the master of Krak d'Entremont. "Too, she could be tethered by means of a cord attached to that ring, and—"

"Woman! Doubtless you have seen women among us with ringèd noses, but you have not seen one during the first few days after her septum is pierced. The entire nose and sometimes more of the face is dark with congesting blood, and swollen. More ugliness! No no. A girl with such a nose would be a bearable couch-partner only in pitch darkness! Nor do I care to wait day after day whilst the swelling abates! Your suggestions are not to my liking, Lovisa."

"I am sorry, Barak," she said, for every time he called her by name without title, she did the same. He needed constant reminders that she was of the nobility, and a useful intimée of Saladin—as intimate as any woman could be. "One supposes the same is true of freshly-ringed nipples, though they do demean a woman yet are pretty to look upon." She used her fingers to make a *ting* sound on one of her slim silver earrings. "And how helplessly she could be bound with the merest of cords, attached to rings through those tiny nipples." *And maybe a nice sudden yank to pull the rings right through and give the soft little ninny four little pink teats!*

"Nay; thou hast said it: the same is true of freshly-pierced nipples, and ugliness. Besides, I am sure that *you* have never felt the cold steel of an unwelcome ring in your mouth, or heard its dinging sound against your teeth!"

"Thou art right: I have not. Ah—both punishment and a softening of her resolve, you said. You have much leather strapping, both cured and rawhide, about. There is this: her torso might be tightly wrapped in wet leather, with only the tiniest of two cracks left for her nipples to peek through, squeezed forth. And squeezed far more drastically, as the

77

leather dries and shrinks on her body."

He smiled. "By the beard of the Prophet, blessings on his reverèd name! Now that is something worth remembering, Lovisa—Lady Lovisa! Aye, and I shall. It is not, however, something to which I wish to resort in this instance, for the straps would mark her body for days and make it as sensitive-unto-pain as the stretching in the sun you suggested." Seeing that she was about to speak, he lifted a hand that glittered with three excellent rings. "No no, I have listened to you enough, my ally. With what are helmets lined, that our heads may be padded from the steel and those blows we might take?"

"Wh-why, sponge from just outside the harbor of Tarsus, lord Barak; they tend to absorb the sweat, too. My lord intends to helmet this girl whose hair is shorter even than a knight's—in the sun, perhaps?"

"I do not, in Allah's holy name! No—a goodly piece of sponge shall be soaked in vinegar, and forced into the mouth of this silly Pau—Rosalba. A cord shall—no, a cord would bite her sweet soft cheeks. A broad strap shall hold it tightly within her face. In addition she shall be bound most uncomfortably, and left to her own means for hours, that she may suffer and *think*." He jerked his white-turbaned head in a single sharp nod. "Aye, by the Suras! So shall it be done!" He eyed his ally speculatively. "Now is it safe to entrust this order to you?—or must I fear that the manner in which you cause her to be bound shall be too stringent, and mark her? For belief is upon me," he said, suddenly pointing an accusing finger, "that for some reason you hold personal dislike for your fellow woman, Lovisa!"

She decided to get a few words said, and looked at the floor as if in demure embarrassment. "I am a woman, and she is a girl, virginally intact. Thou art no unhandsome man and favored by both Allah and Saladin. I have no cause to love her, my good lord. However, I am neither thy enemy nor thy servant, but thy ally who wishes thee only well. Perhaps I shall envy her in your arms, but I shall not betray thee by marking her soft pallid body. I have no desire to incur thy displeasure, Barak-emir."

Again his expression as he gazed at her was speculative. "She is a fascinating trifle, a mere child, for girls do not become women as early among you Franks as among the chosen of Allah! Once I have plucked her flower..." He rose in a rustle of silk and damask trousers tucked into boots of red felt. "Would benefit us both were I to give the orders myself, and with precision, I now see that. You might perhaps wish to cover your snow-capped mountains a bit more thoroughly, and join me anon in an inspection of our upper battlements?"

How cleverly he avoids saying "I do not trust you," she thought, and she said, "Aye, my lord, I shall await your pleasure."

So it was that the mouth of the blonde was well stuffed with new sponge swollen and dripping with vinegar, and a black leathern band tightened about her lower face to hold it in place. To avoid marking that pretty face, Barak specified that the strap be thick and tall enow to cover her from nose to chin. Since her mouth was forced quite wide, the strap gave her a long-faced look. Another band, of softer leather but as thick and wide, formed a collar for her and forced her to keep her chin well up. Already the vinegar was bringing tears to her eyes.

She was made to sit, bare-bottomed on stone, and her ankles strapped and crossed, so that the length that ran around behind her back held each heel right up to her privates—which her position sprung softly open. A simple cuff on each wrist and a strap running across the back of her neck connected them and held her hands up beside her face, arms bent up at the elbows.

She was totally helpless, explicitly open and available,

79

and guaranteed soon to be most uncomfortable indeed. She was also bound so as to be seen by every man who passed. The order would be given: they might stare all they wished, but were not to taunt or touch her. She was the emir's— *first*, he cleverly added.

"After three days," he said for her ears, "give her all the water she can drink and see that she exercises out the kinks that soon will be flames in her muscles!"

Several paces away he quietly issued the real directive: "She is to sit thus for four hours, which may well seem three days to her! At the end of that time, release her— without fondling, do you understand me?—and hand her a waterskin. It is to be filled with wine. Allah knows those accursed Hospitallers had plenty of that on hand!"

"Hear and obey, my lord!"

"Good. The Lady Lovisa and I are going up onto the wall. Pass the word to every lieutenant as to the captive's being stared at, but neither touched nor mocked. He who disobeys will feel the lash."

"Understood, my lord!"

With a brief nod and a swish and flutter of his light silken cloak the color of milk the emir whirled and paced away to fetch Luisa and go above. He wanted this damned girl, and he needed something to keep him occupied while he awaited the pleasure of pushing and pulling her yarn. Her golden yellow Frankish yarn, he thought with a smile, envisioning that small silky thatch at the base of her tiny belly.

He should never have asked *Lady* Lovisa's advice to begin with, he mused. Still, it had been a sort of test, and he must consider that she had passed; certainly she had suggested cruel ordeals Lovisa would hardly care to endure herself! Nevertheless, it had all been a waste of time, albeit somewhat enlightening in more ways than one. This Frankish *lady* Saladin trusted so was imaginative, at least. Or—likelier the word, Barak reflected, was *experienced*. And...

80

And she fancies me, does she? Ho! And by the staff of Allah, that one, I'll wager, is a fine tumble on the couch!

Well, he would find out. Later. First there was the matter of the maiden's maidenhood—and a nunnish one, at that! *Allah will laugh aloud at her virgin's blood, whilst the gods of the Franks weep!*

Luisa wondered why Barak was smiling so pleasantly when she joined him and went up the ladders to the walkways around the top of the walls.

The sun was lowering by the time they had completed most of the circuit and several brief exchanges with respectful guards. Each was strangely—and less than happily—garbed in a cowled black robe of the Order of Hospitallers. Luisa, the "snow-capped mountains" of her breasts hidden beneath a cloak the color of a pigeon's egg, was more than ready to cease this inspection of nothing. Then one of the sentries called softly from an area they had already traversed: the forefront of the castle, overlooking the valley.

The fact that the fellow did not shout told Barak and Luisa that he had spotted someone or someones on the road below, and not Turks. They hurried back to his area of the wall, and this time Barak was so thoughtfully careful as to doff his white-plumed helmet ere he peered out and down.

"Only three men," he murmured. "A knight, his squire, and another; not a knight and yet well-mounted. Hmm—odd. A *mounted archer*, apparently, and with an obscenely long bow! My lady," he said, careful of the proprieties for the benefit of the bright-eyed guard, "wilt thou look? Know thou the device of yon knight?"

Luisa edged up to the crenellation and pushed her head partway through. She looked down into a valley dimmed into twilight and long shadows by the tall hills flanking it. She saw the three riders. Their faces were not distinguish-

81

able and would not have been recognizable even if one had belonged to her own mother.

Nevertheless, she was absolutely certain of the identity of one of them, and a sudden sensation of lightheadedness made her blink and catch her breath.

You silly damned creature—you absolute girl *of an idiot!* she chided herself mentally. *Stop this! That swine of an overgrown peasant spurned you—you! Here is opportunity to see him dead, dead—or better still, delicious thought— a* captive *in this very castle! Miserable, and tortured, and gloated over by . . . me!*

So ran her thoughts, but with a little quiver in her limbs and in her heart she specifically answered the question of Emir Barak: "The knight is French, and serves the Count of Champagne. Otherwise—no, I do not know his armorial bearings, my lord. Dare I go so far as to term him an inconsequential knight? No, I had better not. However, many have been slain and captured in this war, and many is the squire who has gained the spurs of knighthood all on a sudden. I am not likely to remember the colors and devices of such . . . boys."

"You said the Count of Shampanyeh! Him they have made king . . . over a kingdom that does not exist! Hon-ree?" Barak crowded her to look again between the two merlons of stone, and this time excitement was all asparkle in his black, black eyes.

"So I said, my lord, but I did not mean that it is he. It is not. That is the device of Champagne in the corner, thou seest. And the lily of France. They proclaim him a knight of Frankland, and of Champagne. As for the rest . . . well, the arrangement of colors and devices are unknown to me. Beside him rides his squire. The other, as you have noted milord, is but an archer."

I have not lied yet, she thought, while her heart pounded.

"The archers of the Ingländers have such long bows,"

82

Barak said quietly, thoughtfully, and again Luisa did not lie:

"So they do, my lord Emir."

"Shall we feather them and attack, lord?" the sentry asked excitedly. "Three armored enemies of Islam, and see those fine huge horses!"

"I see them," Barak said quietly, as if distracted. "Yet we have no flying squad waiting up the road this time, and in their Frankish armor those men or one of them might well escape us. As yet, the Frank know not that we hold this fortress. This is why you wear that hated robe, Ali. Let us maintain our secret so long as we can, that we can mayhap raid more important parties—larger ones! Aye, Ali, these we let slip through our hands that we may stalk larger game!"

Barak's knuckles paled as his lean brown hand tightened on the leading edge of the crenellated wall. "And hereafter we shall maintain a party of our knights in hiding just up the road from here. I shall ride out myself on the morrow, in quest of the perfect spot for their hiding."

The guard had looked disappointed, but now brightened. "And ambush, my lord Emir!"

"The ambuscade, Ali, shall come from here, in the form of volleys of arrows." Barak's face writhed and his voice was as intense as ever Luisa had heard it. "The cavalry we shall maintain in hiding up yonder... they shall be ever ready to follow up with the annihilating charge!"

Barak drew back, smiling. "So. Those three idolators may never know what prayers they should offer to their many statues of their many gods, that this day they could have died and have been succored by a wise decision—only that more of their accursèd kind may taste our steel! Ride on, three little men of Frankistan, ride on. But come not this way again, lest what has been written concerning your fates be accomplished and you meet your false gods aforetime!"

Luisa stood with a sweat-damp hand to her cloak-covered

bosom. She had never dared try to persuade these people to truth: that Christians, like Muslims, worshiped only one god, and that the statuary and icons and many names were but saints. Because of those many statues and all those names in prayers, all those swear-bys, the Muslims did persist in their belief that Christians were polytheists!

Still, just now that was of no concern, and not in her thoughts:

I have just seen Guy of Messaria, and most likely saved his life when I could as easily have condemned him merely by identifying him! Oh Luisa, you girlish fool! I'd have thought better of you by now, soft-hearted whore!

Another thought came to trouble her, as she and Barak moved away to descend into the castle. They would go down and there would be prayers; these Muslims prayed more than Christians. Then they would sup, and he would rise smiling to array and perfume himself, and go and deflower his new prize. That would leave the Lady Luisa de Vermandois exactly nowhere . . . and already she was damp in her private parts. She knew that she would be even more randy later, for she would not be able to keep her thoughts off Barak and his captive nun.

She refused to admit to herself that it would also not be possible for her to avoid thinking of Guy of Messaria, and that such thoughts would only increase her desire and need of a man.

Damn and damn again! She dared not merely avail herself of one of the many Turks here who gave her such looks, even for an hour; she was determined to have the emir himself, and to bind him to her. She would hardly gain his favor by wallowing with one of his men! *Perhaps this twice-damned place of many men and no available cock has a nice fat cucumber stored away somewhere . . .*

They strolled past the poor bound, gagged nun. She looked terribly uncomfortable, obscenely openly posed, absolutely miserable . . . and unequivocally desirable. Lord Emir Barak ibn-Yusuf al-Daula, Luisa noticed, did not so much as glance at the girl, whose big blue eyes stared at the floor in humiliation and mortification as they passed.

What a clever lovely bastard he is, her fellow Frenchwoman thought.

As he had ordered, the willowy captive had been draped in the headdress of Sister Paulina. It covered her head to the eyebrows while its veil flowed down behind. Denying her any other clothing, he had returned to her the partial cloak of lightweight fabric. Falling just past the middle of her back, the thin fluttery over-garment covered her shoulders and upper arms. As he had known, it would not quite close in front. Nor had this mere girl with her big round sky-colored eyes thought of wearing it hindside to. Thus she might have covered her bosom and, provided she squatted or sat on the floor, her blond-fringed loins as well.

It was not just a woman of the Franks whom Barak ibn-Yusuf had made his prisoner; his men had fetched him a young and shapely nun, one of their holy women, and it was a *nun* he wanted to possess in the sexual embrace. Far more thrill in that than in the use of a mere ordinary girl!

Standing half-crouched in the corner of the chamber farthest from the softly draped couch, she stared at him with fever-bright eyes. One lightly tanned little hand clutched pitifully at that partial cloak in front between her breasts, to cover their pointed eruptions. She leaned forward and down and a bit leftward, since she sought to shield her crotch with her left hand.

Delicious! He showed her a very small smile, while his lecherous gaze slid over her helplessness and the milky whiteness of her legs with their pale, pale down.

He bade her stand straight, and of course she did not understand. Her lips were moving, but he heard nothing.

85

Prayer, he thought. She was praying.

He bade her recline and prepare herself, accompanying the words with an extended arm: his finger pointed at the couch. She glanced at it and shrank even more, seeking to bury her backside in the corner and flow through it out of this chamber with its rug-hung walls, its soft-carpeted floor, the low, filigreed table and ornately carven, backless chair. And its *diwan* or divan, sheeted with white and pale yellow from which dripped yellow tassels gleaming with gold thread.

"Few maidens have such a lovely apartment and such a beautiful soft couch for their defloration," he told her quietly, and of course she understand not a word.

"Oh please, please leave me alone, do not do this, I am wedded to God, I will do anything I can clean and cook and I am good at nursing please..."

Of her murmured string of words he recognized the pleading tone as well as the several uses of *"s'il vous plait"* and *"je"* and *"Dieu"*—which made him scowl and compress his lips—and he understood too her words for "cook" and "nursing." He had learned some of their tongue before Luisa, and had learned more from her, asking the words for this and that and having her say them again and again until he repeated them in a way he thought perfect. So this Rosalba, this *Sister Paulyeeneh*, said "please" several times and "I" several times and called upon her god. Too, she mentioned both cooking and nursing; promising no doubt to do those things for him if only he would leave her that precious bit of skin stretched betwixt her white, white thighs.

"Wee," he said, smiling slightly and nodding. *"Voo cuisinyay, et swanyay, et voo baisay, je baisay."*

Her eyes widened perhaps a bit more as she heard his unexpectedly good pronunciation of "Yes; you cook, and you nurse," and perhaps she was just starting to breathe and consider a tiny smile when he followed with "and you fuck, I fuck..."

86

She slid right to the floor, shaking her head so that her nun's veil hissed and fluttered while she said *"Non, non, non"* again and again and again.

After staring at her for a moment, he paced with a deliberate stride to the couch and seated himself. He stared at her, and with that little smile he said "Yes" in her language every time she said "No."

Then he had a stroke of genius and said, *"Dieu le vult!"*

That shocked her into a staring silence. Both of them had heard those words many times. They formed the rallying cry of the crusaders, and their most frequent battle-cry as well: God Wills It!

She began to weep then, for perhaps it was indeed God's will that she be used as a woman by this dark lion of the desert.

Strangely, it was not too difficult after that. Oh, she shrank away and sought to resist when he rose and fetched her to the couch, and she wriggled and resisted more once she was on it. Yet she was not *fighting*, actually striking at him, so much as she was flailing and striving to wriggle away. When she had subsided a bit, he rose over her with one foot on the floor and one knee on the couch. Again he pointed.

"Stay where you are, Rosalba," he said, and he stripped.

She did not want to look at the revelation of his hard wiry body, and made much show of averting her face and covering her eyes. He did not care. Her hands covered her eyes, aye, and her elbows mostly obscured breasts that he saw were quite stiff, but he gazed at will on her belly and the smooth inward curve of her waist before it flowed out into her hips and round thighs. The centered thatch of blond strands drew his gaze, and the conspicuously bulging purse it did not even pretend to cover. His organ came up, and up, rearing like a roan stallion.

Seating himself on the side of the couch, he slid his hand

up her tight-pressed thighs to that jutting mound. He touched its sparse tendrilly hair like threads of fine silk. Immediately she threw herself onto her side, weeping and quivering. Undaunted, he stroked the upturned flank and the gentle ovals of her bottom. She drew away—to be brought up by the wall on that side of the couch.

This one is not at all violent, he mused, *but like the hare that runs to ground and cowers shuddering rather than trying to fight—as one of* our *women would, of course!*

He stroked the tight-clenched cheeks of her tremulous backside several minutes more than his arousal might have preferred, but her skin was uncommon soft with its close-set little pores. Then he insinuated his fingers between the very tops of her thighs from behind, and touched again the cowering girl's soft-lipped pubis.

At first she lurched, then clamped her thighs together with all her might. Then she flopped again onto her back, trapping his hand under her. He saw that her lips were moving. She was still whispering her prayers. "My Jesus, mercy!" perhaps, or another of their silly litanies.

Smiling into her wet and staring eyes, he laid his other hand on her pubis. For an instant he tickled there with two fingers; then her hands leaped down to grasp his wrist and tug. Immediately the hand beneath her was wriggling a finger between her nether lips. She became eel-like. Flailing her legs, she grasped each of his forearms. He showed her his strength, lifting his hands until she was starting to come up off the bed. She let go, and in that instant he turned his hand and slid his thumb into her. She jerked up to slap at him; he struck that hand away and moved his thumb within the satiny purse of her loins. When she tried to strike again, his forearm was again there.

"Ah, but you are not truly violent, not truly a fighter," he murmured, and she understood not a word.

He flipped her over so that she bounced, face-down.

Within two seconds he had struck both her lovely uprounding buttocks with cupped palms, hard. The twin smacking noises resounded sharply from the walls.

"Thus surely is the fight driven from you, little rabbit," he said aloud, and again she understood none of it. Yet she twisted, jerked, flung herself over, and he was ready and waiting.

Now the futilely resisting girl squealed and jerked wildly at feel of his big hot male organ at the small, tightly clenched mouth of her vagina.

"So much for your troublesome maidenhead," he said, and pushed swiftly into that furnace, in one hard long lunge that hurt his achingly taut erection.

That hard-driving battering ram smashed the gates, breached the delicate barrier of her girlhood, and reduced it to torn and bleeding ruins. She cried out and went rigid in tension. She heard the sloppy sucky noises of her own hymeneal blood and had no idea that there was other lubricant there as well; she and sexuality and her body were strangers. How could there be lubricant present, when it felt as if he had put a knife up her tight virginal track?

Her muscles contracted wildly, or tried to, and that added to the pain so that realization hit Rosalba Giles'-daughter that it would be better if she relaxed.

Ah, but on the other hand, the mind of Sister Paulina intervened . . . should she not feel pain, be punished for allowing this evil act to be perpetrated upon her?

It was not as if she had a choice; it hurt anyhow. Her mouth resumed its silent movements. *Sweet Jesus, mercy! Mary Mother of God, give me strength!*

Abruptly ashamed not to be resisting, she swung up both fisted hands. The lusting Turk was ready even for that. He caught each wrist and pressed them down to the bed on either side of her head. Thus their pose became a classic one, his and hers. She sprawled on her back, stuck up the

89

middle, hands held down, palms up so as to frame her head. She stared piteously up at him. And her lips moved in that constant sibilance he could only just hear.

She was surprised that he did not move like the rutting animal he was; instead he was still, with his flaming and distended member buried up in her belly, soaking in her. It felt as if it had sharp edges, that entrenched organ.

This was not what she had been told about tupping! It was a violent act; she knew it! Why was he so still, on her and in her, with his dark, dark face looming over hers with such intensity in those eyes like basalt?

My Jesus, mercy! Sweet mother of God, strengthen me. Sweet Jesus, mercy...

After a while she could feel the pulse beating in the rigidly swollen flesh imbedded in her body. At the same time she realized that the pain had abated. A minute dragged by in that eerie motionlessness, while his turgidly dilated lance throbbed away inside her, and then another long minute.

So strange... what was he waiting for?

Tentatively she tried twisting her head and her arms. He held them. She gasped at a new flash of pain when he began moving, tugging his loins backward, drawing what felt like a yard-long heated sword out of the tightly sucking mouth of her belly. Her mouth came open and she gasped. She squeezed shut her eyes, turned her face to one side. A tremor flowed through her and her parted mouth trembled. Still her pink lips formed silent words. It had become automatic. She was hardly aware that she continued her standard words begging for sustenance and fortitude. Her heart was pounding wildly and every nerve in her body had come alive.

Easing back until only the broad head of his cock remained ensconced just within her petal-soft lower lips, he repeated his secret exercise: he counted mentally to seventy, holding back his raging body with considerable prideful effort.

Anyone, he told himself, *can rape! The lowest beast of a crusading Christian swine can rape—and does! I am Barak ibn-Yusuf al-Daula. I do not rape: I fuck a nun with regard for her virginal discomfort, and put the lie to her beliefs and expectations as I do to her celibacy and vows!*

He worked his hips then, just a little, making only the crown of his erection move within the softly clasping purse of her labia.

"You are like silk inside," he said quietly, and she understood nothing. He saw that her lips continued to move, forming words without sound.

Again he moved his hips, this time insinuating perhaps an additional half-inch of his body into hers. She twitched and gasped.

"Before I cease plumbing your pussy, you too shall be moving," he told her quietly. "You may even cease your idiotic praying," he added, and again the blonde knew not a word he spoke. She could only lie staring up at him from within her nunnish headdress and veil, the snug headband covering her down to the eyebrows like a tight-fitting helmet of white.

"Into . . . you," he said, and pushed in, long and slow.

He accompanied the thrust with a small lateral movement of his hips, easing and cruising up between soft puffy lips and into the liquid inner heat of her. She did not know his words, but he understood her:

"uh . . ."

He pushed steadily until his cock was enveloped in the cloying heat of satiny tissues and his bollocks lay against her while the jet tendrils of his pubic hair, hardly so silken as hers, curled at her open cleft. She made other soft sounds in response to the pressure she felt inside her.

This time he counted, silently and secretly, only to fifty before easing himself out of her.

Raising his body over hers, he looked down between

91

them. He saw his headless shaft, looking darker than usual pressed against the pale-furred pink lips of this Frankish nun, and he saw the blood of her shredded hymen. It was a good sight, all of it, and beyond exciting. He moved his hips, circling, watching his movements, watching the way the end of his prick changed the shape of her labia as it moved between them...

And he drove back into her with slamming power that tensed her belly and made her eyes flair and brought a whimpering cry from her.

Her taut, upstanding breasts were heaving as if flaunting their pale pink buds. Liquid noises rose from the joining of their bodies and a great shudder trembled through the girl's prostrate nakedness. He thrust in hard and rocked his hips, having babied and gentled her all he could bear; now he squirmed atop the moaning blonde to drive the head of his cunt-wet staff against her cervix. His black eyes stared down into the pale, liquid azure of hers, which were huge and round. A final wrinkle gave way somewhere inside that cringing crevice, so that his cock slid in farther. That let his balls slap the flesh of her perineum, and she gasped and licked her lips anxiously, tensing as he achieved his goal. He watched another great shudder flow through her. Her lips trembled and he knew that now she could not get them together.

"You are wearing me," he said low in his language, "wearing me on you and inside you, my Frankish nun, my pale-haired Rosalba!"

She blinked and shuddered at the sound of her former name from his lips.

The swollen bulb of his prick had thumped with a jar into the neck of her uterus so that she grunted at the pressure. He was straining to hold it there, feeling the pressure on the very tip of his organ almost as pain, yet still pushing as if attempting to drive the whole iron-hard shaft up her

92

womb, up into the very belly of her. She groaned and grunted, lying beneath him: virginal, a nun, and stuffed full of Saracen cock. Her mouth hung loosely open. The lips no longer moved in prayer.

Defensively, the thick, luscious fluid of her inner cunt enfolded the big shaft driven so roughly into her, entrenched so deeply in her.

Grinding it in, he seemed trying to nail her arse to the bed with the spike of his loins. He had lowered himself to her, so that beneath his grinding chest now he could feel the throbbing hardness of her nipples, stuck on the ends of her upthrusting titties like knobs to tease him. He knew the message of those tautened nipples: she was aroused.

His thick erection wallowed deep in the slushy heat of her, and she was aroused!

He trembled with an inner excitement of intensified lechery, pure lechery and lust for her, for her body, for her pale western skin and her snugging wet pussy, for her passion. He would have it, he told himself as he moved once more, swaying his hips to make his entrenched staff bang about within her, daunting the taut muscular clasp of a furrow never before even challenged.

He pulled and pushed, pulled and pushed, threw fucking movements at her three and then four times, very rapidly.

She moaned and shuddered, looking piteously up at him, twitching her head aside to stare at the wall, then turning back to look up at his looming dark face once more. A new tautness in the hot pink caps of her breasts prodded up against the plates of his chest, pink into deep, deep tan. He moved his shoulders to grind down on those fine firm white titties and felt a new shiver flow throughout her lean young body.

She could actually feel curling, crisp hairs against her sensitive nipples. She wished that it was a horrible sensation, and was mortified that it was not.

He moved, moved. His big sword of flesh stabbed between her blood-gorged sex-lips, again and again. She was moving, just a little; he was almost sure of it...

Looming over her, he watched the fucked (and fucking?) girl bite her lip while he stuffed frothing plugging erection up her, up her, all the way inside. Her cunt took it, and there was no pain in her face. God, O God, the way her newly-opened vaginal vise clutched at him, as if lovingly!

With a fierce, hungry drive he punched into that warm, warm pocket that seemed to have no bottom. He sought one.

His hips pounded hers unmercifully. His hairy thighs flailed between hers, so sleek and pale and round, taut with the musculature of youth. He watched her eyes glaze over and become luminous. Hearing the rapid heavy gasps of her breath, he knew his own was the same. Shiver after shiver rippled the glossy-smooth, pearly shimmer of her skin, so excitingly pale. His body glided and flailed hers now, his cock whipping in and out with slickened ease. The craving organ was drawn into a raging vortex that quivered and writhed under his driving body. In that soft and fleshy dwelling place, his entrenched staff twitched so that he moaned. He ground his hips, hearing the wet noises of liberated woman-juices bathing his deep-rooting cock.

Ah, name of Allah but it sounded good, felt good!

His guts were squirming in the grip of almost unendurable passionate pleasure. How good it felt, how good! And then suddenly he wanted to laugh. The totally involuntary jerking of her body filled the quivering, sap-saturated sleeve of her vagina with every inch of his churning staff, and massaged it!

She felt that robust poker bulging the tensile walls of her cunt in a way that sent hot sensations whipping all through her. She had no idea that she was squirming so hard. Her sagging mouth trickled little mewling sounds and her eyes were glassy.

Hips that were at once broad and yet lean quivered as he punched deeply between them into the hot, inviting reaches of her. Her nunnish vagina was a torrid pit of hot gravy that clenched and swirled around him. Repeatedly he tightened his arsecheeks and plunged into the sheathing, raging womanfire while his chest ground over her breasts, challenging their upstanding youthful firmness. The need for release was building in him, building, rising. It was a mounting pressure in his guts and his balls.

Still holding each of her wrists clamped while he rooted in her, he decided to release her. He did. Crossing his arms before him, under his chest, he grasped each of her breasts and pressured them toward each other. She gasped, but made no move to thwart him. God Whose Name is Allah, how stiff and taut they were! What girlishly hard and muscular projections this unusual girl's titties were, like additions stuck into her narrow chest after the rest of her was completely formed!

An afterthought of God's, he mused; *and He did good work with her, even though He added these knobs after He had formed the rest of her!*

Meanwhile he loved watching and feeling the way the sprawled blonde quaked so constantly. Shivers rocked her with the goading, goaded sensation in her splayed-open cleft. The big throbbing cylinder of flesh was buried deep in her belly, tearing away at her cunt so that she burned with it.

Sprawling on her, deliberately giving her all his weight, he swiveled his hips and lunged with tightened buttocks. The cords in his neck stood out in prolonged sexual tension while his sex-aroused shaft flew in and out of the burrow he had opened and widened.

Cock-stroking hard, he began to tremble, stiffening ...

95

and then he was groaning aloud through an open mouth, nearly crying out as climactic release struck. It struck hard. He jerked, grinding in, out of control. For the first time since the breaching of her hymen she gave voice to a cry, for she felt it happening.

Powerfully spurting jets shot from him with the force of a volley of arrows. Turkish arrows, volleying into Christian flesh. His thick semen splashed off the quaking walls of her vagina. She felt it, felt the strange new sensation of it spurting into her. A sort or rictus rocked her. Similarly, his whole body shook as he relieved himself of that vital elixir and sent it flooding from his body into hers.

Then, emptied, he sagged gasping onto her. He lay that way, weak and vulnerable but sure that he had nothing to fear from this girl, this former virgin (and former?) nun.

He did not leave her at once. He spent time lying upon her, stroking her, pressing kisses onto her nipples, shifting to the side to take part of his weight from her well-ridden body while his cock soaked in their combined fluids inside her and slowly withered to a small softness. She lay not quite as if dead, but doubtless willing herself not to respond or touch him with her little hands.

Perhaps she felt only horror and disgust, or shame; perhaps even hatred. Perhaps, he mused, she was not a sexual being. Some who entered holy orders among both his religion and hers felt no sexual need, or denied it. Nunnish habits and priestly or monkish garb and rules formed a haven and shelter for such people. Some were frightened of the world. Some feared sex and sexuality, even their own. He had no idea why this Sister Paulina, this Rosalba of the Franks, had fled the real world to enter that artificial and unnatural one of a convent—and when she was yet so young, so attractive and well-made. Some disappointment in love, peradventure. A fear of sexuality though she knew naught

96

of it, mayhap? He knew that such was not uncommon among the *Nazareni,* the Christians.

Barak did not care much. Further, he thought that while she had felt horror and might now feel some disgust and shame, she did not hate him. Nor did he believe her to be a nonsexual being—as his first but definitely not his second wife was, back in Damascus. Barak ibn-Yusuf—son of Joseph—was experienced, and knew women. He had felt response in this girl of Frankistan, seen it lurking behind her eyes. He was sure that it had been there and that she had denied and fought and suppressed it. That was natural enough. At last, with a long sigh, he rose from her.

"Tu est beau, et bon," he said, looking down into her blue, blue eyes and hoping he had it right in her language: "You are beautiful, and good."

She said nothing and did not move while he resumed his clothing. *"Je suis Malek Barak ibn-Yusuf,"* he told her, and bent to kiss her nipple. She gasped and averted her face. He let the chamber of her imprisonment.

Soon he was issuing quiet orders:

"Take her a basin and soft cloth, that she may wipe and comfort herself. Also a bit of scented oil she might use to soothe her parts. Wine, too, and tender sweetmeats. You have this?"

"Yes my lord," his chief lieutenant and aide said, with a brief bob of his unhelmeted but white-turbaned head. Small and of gold, his single earring flashed with the movement of his head.

"Good. And then, after a time, Mahmud, do you go to her again. I bid you—I *command* you to be both firm and gentle. Do not rape her: make love to her, but when you enter her, fuck as a man fucks, as you do. Caress her a bit after you have pumped into her, rather than merely rolling off and hurrying to perform your cleaning ablutions as the prophet, his name be blessed, commands. Ah yes, smile, you rascal!" The emir lifted an instructive finger. "As you leave her, uncork a vial of perfume in her chamber, that she may have pleasure of scented air. Next, send a bit of honey to her, in my name. And then, after another while, give these same instructions to Shawar as orders from me, so that he too goes to her and into her. He is to give her some trifling garment; merely a turban winding, perhaps, that she may use on her body as she wishes. And a fresh cloth for her wiping. You have all this in your head, Mahmud?"

"Aye, my lord!" Mahmud's teeth flashed in a delighted smile. "She is to be fucked again and again, but not brutalized and always given some trifling gift."

"You have it. We treat her as a valued woman rather than as a holy 'woman' or infidel. And have the water removed and fresh provided," he said, for the castle's well was deep, and far from empty. "A fresh cloth for her own ablutions, as well. Again, give her considerable time to rest. After that it is to be al-Athir's turn with her, and in the same wise. She is not to be brutalized, or merely raped. He is to provide her with a coverlet, and send an orderly to *treat her politely* and replace the sheet on the divan—her divan."

Mahmud was nodding. "Aye, my lord. And then . . . Yusuf, my lord?"

Barak showed the other man a tiny smile. "No. Four is enough for a virgin and a nun to accommodate on the night of her defloration! It is the price Yusuf must pay for his indulgence; my fattest lieutenant shall have to wait."

Mahmud chuckled while he nodded. Barak allowed his little smile to broaden into a grin. He clapped a hand to Mahmud's powerful shoulder, squeezed, and left the fortyish soldier-noble of Islam to gaze, smiling, after his tall emir's fluttering yellow cloak.

* * *

Luisa had at last got to sleep. A goodly portion of wine had helped make relaxation possible; she had further aided herself by rubbing her prominent clitoris to two orgasms, pinching herself the while so that her right nipple would be touch-sore all the morrow, and gouging several fingers as far into herself as she could. Sprawled naked, she slid at last into sleep and lay in abandon. Buried deep in the castle of stone, her chamber was at least not hot.

She awoke with a start to find an oil-lamp lit on the little rough-hewn table of the ascetic Hospitallers. In its pallid light she looked up to see Barak standing over her. The muzziness of sleep left her and she let him see that she was not merely staring, but glaring. Still, she said nothing about her privacy or his intrusion. Nor did she make any attempt to cover her nudity.

"My lady. The nun is no longer nun, or virgin either. Other men will visit her this night, as well."

That latter part of his declaration surprised her, and pleased her. Then he did not after all intend to make that little nothing of a girl his sole property and . . . toy?

"She is a pale and smallish wisp, fearful and quaking, who prayed silently all the while," he told her, with only a small prevarication. "It was a fuck, nothing more, and scarce worth the God-commanded ablutions I must perform after. This I have just done. Along about now my aide Mahmud al-Khalani is going to her, and into her. It will give him release, at least. And then . . ." His careless gesture showed that he spoke of nothing of importance. "My other lieutenants, Shawar and Al-Athir. A gift from their emir, and a release for their natural needs."

Luisa reached negligently for a bit of muslin coverlet, with gelatinous movements of her awe-inspiring chest. "This is of some mild interest, but why does my lord rouse me to tell me now?"

Standing over her bed, he gazed steadily down at her. "I

have indulged myself and had a girl, a squealy virgin. It reminded me of what a woman is like. Methinks thou art a woman, Lady Lovisa my ally. This I say at the risk of offending thee," he said, as if it were not he who held the power here.

The power was his, and she did not even consider being less than receptive, much less to sneer or deny him.

Besides, she did not want to.

In a very soft voice she said, "What woman could be offended by the attentions of Barak ibn-Yusuf?"

He reached down to close a hand over her nearer breast, the right. How much there was of that soft, outsize pomegranate! His fingers sank in and he tugged. Concealing her wince and determined not to let him know how sensitive she had already made that heavy and massive melon, she allowed herself to be pulled into a sitting position. Her hands went to his hips.

"My lord and lover is overdressed," she murmured.

Those who were present there assured
Us that they danced through the late hours
Of night, their heads bedecked with flowers
Entwined in garland and in crown;
Beside wine casks they sat them down
And drank until morning bells had rung;
Then homeward made their way among
The harlots . . .

—AMBROISE (NORMAN MINSTREL),
writing of the French in Tyre in
History of the Holy War

SIX

The Siege of Darum

A bit under thirty miles south of Tyre, the town of Akka or Acre crouched on the coast of the Mediterranean. Here had begun this Crusade of Kings, and Acre with its mighty defensive tower had been a long, long time afalling to the Christians.* About sixty miles below Acre, Jaffa brooded over the sea. Barely over twenty miles southeast of Jaffa sprawled the holy city of Jerusalem, goal of the crusades and yet Holy City also to their Muslim enemy. It had become Saladin's southern capital, rather than Damascus so far to the north.

Due south down the coast from Jaffa rose the walls of Ascalon, and still twenty miles farther south was well-fortified Darum. Lord Saladin's Turks still held Darum, and for several reasons Richard the Lion-heart wanted the town.

He had spent Easter at Ascalon, with his sister and others. Immediately afterward, even as he reconnoitered Darum and Gaza, came dreadful news from his justiciar in England. There dwelt the Lion-heart's younger brother, John Lack-lands. (Although his royal brother had given him suzerainty over much of England, so that the "lack" was hardly true.) While England's king was negotiating with Saladin and plotting against his holdings, young John was also indulging himself in some plotting . . . against his older brother. Meanwhile, in Europe King Philip of France had set aside the

*Detailed in *The Accursed Tower*, the first book of the Crusader's adventures

oaths he had sworn to Richard, along with his honor: Philip was showing a definite interest in Richard's lands.

It was maddening, frustrating. Richard was urged to return to England, and he wanted to; if he remained here, what might become of his kingdom in England and his ducal holdings abutting Philip's lands? Yet if he left, he would be abandoning the militarily successful crusade he led, and he knew that he would ever after be blamed and criticized. Should Saladin succeed in destroying or putting to flight the half-led "army" and tiny Christian kingdom its royal leader would have left behind, the blame would be laid on Richard called "Yea or Nay" and of course "lion-heart."

On the other hand... suppose by some miracle those Richard left behind accomplished the goal of making treaty with Saladin, or soundly defeating his forces and gaining Jerusalem? All Christendom would note and laugh over the fact that once King Richard left, the war went well...

And so the harried lion with the red-gold mane sent messengers to his agents and regents, and remained on in this inhospitable land in which even the very weather seemed on the side of the enemy. Next came news of the murder of Conrad, and then he had to deal with the marriage and ascension of Henry of Champagne.

While the Lion-heart perhaps dreamed of riding his big horse into Jerusalem, he allowed rumors to trickle out that he would move against the fortress of Ildris. Meanwhile he planned an assault on Darum. To that end he had sent messages to the Duke of Burgundy and the Count of Champagne, urging both to hasten their French forces southward to join him. He waited... and then he sent them another message...

Richard's fellow Norman, Ambroise the minstrel, wrote angrily and scathingly of the pleasure-taking French up in Tyre. Meanwhile his lion-hearted lord fumed and strove to hold together a divided and seemingly doomed crusade, even to further its holy purpose. Each new problem that arose among his barons, each day that passed without the advent of the French, made him wish the more that he were where he should be: back in England, back in Normandy, seeing to his own business and most probably reveling in weather and combat he knew about and loved.

Into this moil, in late May, rode Guy Kingsaver with Sir Vulgrin and the latter's squire, Radulph. They were welcomed with smiles and delighted shouts. Many a man was astonished to see the tall, tall king embrace the big youth who had saved his life in a Cyprian stable and served him— and them all—so well in the year that had passed since. That night and its events had preserved King Richard's life, and changed the life of Guy Peter's son forever.

Guy Kingsaver was unusually tall, at six feet; nevertheless King Richard was taller by two inches, with a breadth of shoulder and length of arm that made his ax or sword the nemesis of any enemy within two yards. As he bent one of those long arms slightly, its hand on Guy's shoulder, Richard smiled.

"You are fully recovered, Guy?"

"Aye, lord king. I was ready to join you here before the physician would allow me to rise from bed."

"Ah well, we must needs always obey those healers," the lion-heart said, who had never fully obeyed a physician's instructions in his life. "What news?"

"We rode here without so much as seeing a Saracen. With me is Sir Vulgrin, whom the Count of Champagne knighted less than a month agone. He was squire to Sir—"

"Yes, yes. You said 'the Count of Champagne.' Is it truth then that my nephew is not styling himself as King of Jerusalem?"

"It is true, lord king. And more—his instructions are that none shall call him that. However, my lord king will be pleased to hear something I noticed: Count Henry is in command. My lady Queen defers to him and his judgment."

"Good. Is he following close behind you?"

"I . . . think not, lord king. He has had much to do since his ascension, of course, and awaits the arrival of milord of Burgundy and his men."

"Damn and God's balls! Waiting for that damned Hugh— he was not in Tyre when you left, then? And when he does arrive, he will find reasons to delay . . . while his men fuck away their energies in the arms of Tyre's whores! Devil rot them all!" Richard banged his big right fist into his left palm. "That does it, then. I have grown worse than weary of waiting. The army grows worse than restless, and you are here with us. Sir Vulgrin shall just have to represent the French, by Holy Rood! We shall move come morning, and strike at Darum whilst Saladin expects me elsewhere. You bring despatches, Guy?"

"Aye, lord king," the Crusader said, and hefted the oiled leather bag.

"Good, then. Find yourself a tent—no, no need to bother. We move on the morrow. You will night in my pavilion, Guy." The king raised his voice. "Sir Vulgrin! England and Normandy bids you halloo and welcome! It seems that you and a few others already here represent all of France."

Vulgrin flushed and smiled. "Thank you, my lord. I can but hope that I am worthy!"

"We have no doubt of it!" Richard called back. Then he muttered, only for his ears and Guy Kingsaver's, "You could be worthy of France if you were one-armed and crippled, boy." Suddenly he waved the despatch bag on high and raised his voice to a battlefield bellow: "Messages from Champagne, the new king of Jerusalem! Soon he and Burgundy and all their French will join us!"

Some men cheered; many did not. The greatest noise, naturally, came from the smallish grouping of tents and pavilions above which flew French banners.

"Edwin Long-arm! Bernart! Yves—attend me. Guy: do you greet your friends and join me after vespers."

The king swung away then, and Guy was sure that he was forgotten for the moment. "Yves! Advise the barons and Anselm the Templar to consult with me. Bernart—see that weapons are sharpened and men ready to march at dawn."

The burly man looked happy. "Aye, sire!"

"Boost their morale by spreading word of the great prowess of this new knight of France who arrived with Guy of Messaria—what's his name, Guy?"

"Sir Vulgrin—of Montmirail."

"Vulgrin, Vulgrin. A great fighter, Bernart. Oh—let your lads know that any man who forsakes camp to visit one of those accursed camp-followers this night will suffer my wrath on the morrow. Ah, Edwin, here you be. Greet Guy and go about among your men with him, that they may be of better cheer. We cease this hen's piss inaction on the morrow, with matins."

Without awaiting acknowledgements of his orders from the two men-at-arms, the tall king swung away. He strode toward the sprawling pavilion under his triple-leopard banner of scarlet.

Guy stood looking after him with a little smile. It was a small lie, after all, to rouse the morale of the men, this invented business of untested Vulgrin's mettle! What a great leader of men was Ricart Rex of Angeleterre!

"Guy?" Bernart said, a thick, auburn-bearded man who was master of Richard's foot-soldiery: the men-at-arms. "You were wounded, I heard."

"Aye, but hale now, Bernart. The men are restless? Dispirited?"

"Ah, they need only to move and fight—get the blood up, by Saint Withold! Come, let us be about showing you to them."

Guy nodded and accompanied the sergeant among the grizzled men-at-arms. All greeted him by name. Whether they knew him or not, they knew of him and recognized the youthful hero. In returning their greetings, he said the names of as many as he could. Some had questions.

"Is't true you saved the life of Count Henry, Guy?"

"Aye. Was an easy task, Dickon. There was only one man," Guy said, and dropped his voice to add, "and he was a noble."

These leather-clad commoners of England and Normandy laughed at that; it was they who were slain the most in combat, for the nobles were mounted and nigh invulnerable in their mail. Besides, if one were overcome he was seldom slain but was taken prisoner whenever possible, to be returned in exchange for some ransom or other. No one paid ransom for a commoner.

"And Conrad? Ye tried to save his arse as well, and took a wound thereby?"

Guy nodded. "True. There was more than one assailant that time, and they were dangerous men . . . not nobles."

More laughter, and a mailed blond said, "Methinks I should pretend that I had been wounded in the service of Count Henry rather than that Italian whoreson!"

Guy shrugged. "He was king. Well, he be dead now, and I'll not speak ill of him. Will, wherever did you steal that handsome coat of scale-mail?"

The Lincolnshireman smiled and moved his shoulders in an exaggerated preening movement. "Earned it, by the Cross! I ran a lance right up into the crotch of the Saracen knight who wore it. That be the way to kill 'em when they be mounted and all shining and arrogant, ye see. Stick the bastards low so as not to spoil their pretty armor with their pukish blood!"

"Well done!" Guy called with a laugh. He slapped that mailed shoulder and immediately pretended to have hurt his hand, so that men laughed. "As you are my friend I must say this, though: every Turk will want to remove the head of the man he sees wearing the armor of a dead comrade."

"Hmm," Bernart said, frowning. "Will, there be truth in that. Mayhap—"

Seeing how straw-haired Will's long homely face was falling, Guy interrupted: "Mayhap ye could be wearing a light leathern coat *over* that mail, Will, in combat. Sort of a disguise, ye see. Oh, your pardon, Bernart," he added, pretending that he had not deliberately interrupted before the sergeant could decide that Will and the Turkish mailcoat should part company.

"Passing good advice, by'r Lady. Will, see that ye do as Guy recommends, so that ye live past the morrow. Guy, come over here, now, and see our Richard's Pretty Girl . . ."

Guy was led to inspect a mangonel. Extremely heavy-looking, the siege engine's rectangular frame was equipped with four wooden wheels. Uprights at the center of the frame supported a thick, rounded crosspiece that back-curved at each end so as to resemble an archer's bow. The main aspect of the weapon was a long vertical pole thick as a man's waist. It ended in a big cup-shape of wood and leather; a cup capable of holding a two-hundred-pound boulder or other missiles.

While bows and catapults operated on the principle of tension to hurl their missiles, the mangonel's propelling force came from a combination of tension and torsion. A long windlass across the rear of the frame wound taut a huge rope that dragged the cup back and down, while a smaller, twisted rope from the bow-shaped crosspiece provided resistance in an attempt to hold the cup's pole in place. On release of both tension and torsion simultaneously, the pole lunged upright with terrific impetus. It also slammed against the bow-like crosspiece and sent its missile hurtling up and out with enormous force. The missile was directed either against a fortress's walls or over them, to fall within. There it smashed structures—and anyone within or even around them.

Some said that a knight on horseback could smash through the very walls of Babylon. Well, perhaps . . . so long as the way was prepared for him by mangonels, catapults, and perhaps trebuchets—and miners to tunnel under walls. A charging war-horse could work up to a gallop as fast as a mangonel-loosed missile, but no horse would smash into a wall so as to crack and weaken it and bring down stone and mortar!

"This looks meaner than the mangonel King Philip called *Malvoisin*—'Bad Neighbor,'" Guy commented.

"And so it be," Bernart said, trying to scratch under the scalloped piece of boiled leather he wore to cover chest and shoulders. "That genius we call our lord Richard has added a brace of improvements. This'un he's named Pretty Girl. See the X-frame, here within the main framework, for increased sturdiness, and . . ."

Three days later, under a baking sun, Guy Kingsaver watched Pretty Girl slam an enormous boulder at the wall of Darum.

The missile was lighter than the previous stone and went high because some harried engineer had failed to make new allowances and readjust. It crashed into the very top of the wall with a frightful noise and a spray of stone fragments, mortar and dust—and no fewer than two defenders. One was seen to fly into the air, his arms flailing, and fall back inside Darum; the other pitched up and over, bright red balloon-pants fluttering, to slam meatily to the ground outside, ten or twelve feet from the base of the wall.

Having crunched off the tops of two merlons, the stone went on to topple into the fortress city. The mass of besieging crusaders heard the crash as some building was flattened or at least horribly holed.

"Rottennn!" a voice bawled, and the engineer in charge of Pretty Girl cringed, for the voice was that of Richard Lion-heart. "Weigh your stones, man, and adjust for lighter ones with more arc! It's the wall we want to crack, not a merlon or two and an outhouse inside!"

The red-faced engineer ground his teeth. Naturally he knew every bit of that. It was just that he had slipped, this once. The sun was truly a baker's oven today and every man was losing water by the pint. Besides, a mangonel was no precision weapon. It needed big targets. A stone of unusual shape could easily catch air and go low or astray, even loft a bit. Ah, if only all stones were uniformly round, or if only a man had a huge supply of big iron balls!

"Tortoise out—I want that Paynim corpse!" the king's bawling voice rose again.

Half a dozen men went within a peaked-roof shelter twenty feet long and laid hold of it on the inside. They began trundling the tortoise noisily forward on eight wheels, each composed of two braced and bolted semicircles of wood. From within Darum's walls archers commenced sending flaming arrows whistling down at that mobile shell of a shield for many men. Since it was covered with strips of hide kept well-wetted, the Turks failed in their attempt to set it ablaze.

Guy Kingsaver raised his eyebrows, seeing how one defender exposed himself in a large crenel or embrasure, to aim his pitch-dipped arrow. He must have noted a space in the hides, Guy thought, and reached for the long, long bow that so far no other man had been able to pull. He nocked an arrow and considered breeze and elevation. Once again he demonstrated why he had earned the jocularly respectful title "the Human Crossbow."

His arrow hummed up like an angry wasp and, dropping a bit low, took the Saracen archer in the thigh.

The yellow-surcoated fellow screamed and staggered. Flailing, he tried to save himself from falling backward off the platform within the wall. He overcompensated. With another cry, he pitched out and down to join his comrade on the ground between wall and the besieging host.

Cheers rose from many Christian throats amid the noise of the tortoise's wooden wheels ... and then a new kind of shout arose. A single knight was charging the wall!

His sword was still in its scabbard. Carrying no lance and wearing the white surcoat of a crusader so that he was not even identifiable, he must have gone mad to make such a lunatic charge.

Yet even as he galloped in close to the wall and arrows skittered off his helmet and mailcoat or lodged in his shield or the rings of his mail, he proved that he was hardly mad.

His gauntleted hands loosed a big coil of rope. One end was turned a time or three around his saddle bow; at its other end large hooks swung, black and evil in the sunlight. Their needly points dropped onto the first corpse. The knight, first seen as manic and now as incredibly valiant, swerved his mount and came galloping back, bent low, dragging the body with the grapnel's rope snaking tautly back from his saddle bow.

Three several arrows stood out of his back and one quivered in his arm, and yet he felt none of them. The steel rings of his silver-gleaming armor were set too close to allow the full arrowhead to enter. His hauberk or quilted underjacket, however, had grasped the points. Many a Frank had gained such mementoes without a wound; many a Saracen had fallen to one of his own arrows, plucked forth and returned by the crusader archers.

Only Guy of Messaria—and a fellow named Radulph— recognized the armored knight in the plain white surcoat of a crusader over standard linked chain, for he wore one of the newer head-encompassing helmets. The iron pot totally concealed his face. Guy recognized the green-and-blue plume on that helm, and he knew that saddle, too. He was astonished, for newly knighted Vulgrin of Montmirail had no opportunity to display his manic bravery on their ride here. This was the young man Richard had called hero only so as to cheer the men—and now Vulgrin was proving him right!

"Vulgrinnnn!" Guy suddenly remembered to bellow. "Sir Vulgrin of Montmirail! Up Sir Vulgrinnn!"

Naturally others took up the cry, many with no notion as to what a Vulgrin was.

Dashing back to his own ranks on his snorting destrier, Vulgrin loosed the rope so that the dead Turk he had hooked rolled over and over to flop to a stop at the very feet of the tall man with the red-gold hair. Even as Richard started to smile, Vulgrin was urging his horse on. Men lurched aside. And there was Radulph awaiting him—with another pair of grappling hooks on a long thickrope. A gauntleted hand snatched it; a powerful arm tensed and twitched rein, and the plunging horse swerved sharply to go galloping back toward the wall.

A glance upward showed Richard that more archers in spiked helmets were appearing in the embrasures between Darum's merlons, determined to slay the man who flaunted his disregard for them and their arrows—and so dishonored their dead comrade. The king's bellow rose louder than Guy's, calling for a volley.

Seconds later a dark cloud rushed up from the crusading ranks, so many arrows that their awful scream as they cut the air was audible to every man. Turkish archers ducked or died. A few got off their bowshots, and more arrows whistled down at the galloping knight.

Gone all cold and businesslike, Guy Kingsaver moved mechanically. His long and incredibly powerful bow sent shaft after feather-tipped shaft up at those bowmen, and three of four hurriedly-chosen targets felt the bite of his arrowheads. None fell outside the wall.

Leaning well out of his cradling saddle, Vulgrin slung loose his rope. The awful hooks trailed as his horse carried him toward the second falling Turk. An arrow rang on his helm and went skimming harmlessly away. Slowing his mount a trifle, he slung his grapnel. One or more of the hooks caught in the Paynim body, and the youthful knight was spurring back toward his comrades with the dead man dragging behind his destrier. Arrows rushed past, fell about him. Another swarm of arrows rushed up from the Frankish lines toward the archers of Darum.

The Turks bellowed and screamed their rage and their curses. Two of their slender death-shafts glanced off Vulgrin's armor and two more off that of his mount. Another slammed into the knight's back and stuck there, quivering. He did not notice. His horse's hooves trailed dust in twin plumes that became one and almost obscured the corpse dragging along behind the big bay. Thousands of eyes watched. He reigned in as he approached the tall figure of the unhelmeted king, and only at his mailed feet did Vulgrin let the body come to a halt. He put up both hands to hoist the heavy, sponge-lined steel cylinder off his head then, and bowed his bare head to Richard. Sweat plastered the brown locks to the young knight's head, and ran down his face.

"You wear no mailed coif within your new helm, sir knight?"

Vulgrin showed no surprise that Richard's first words to him were an expression of curiosity or perhaps disapproval, rather than congratulations and thanks. The young man answered quietly, looking a little embarrassed.

"I cannot bear it, lord king, in this heat. The helmet suffices."

"For myself, I cannot bear those iron pots! Why does

your valiant horse wear only a plain cloth of green and leathern armor, sir knight? None even knew who you were, saving only him that rode here with you."

"I . . . lord king, I am making no attempt to hide my identity—it just was not important whether I was recognized. I was having a caparison made for my destrier, with my bearings, but my lord of Champagne sent me to you ere the seamstress was finished. I have not long worn knightly spurs, lord king."

"Is your mailcoat not equipped with a coif, then, sir hero?"

"Lord king, it is not."

Richard reached out to place a big hand on the young Frenchman's mailed thigh. "What you did was most valiant and most unwise, Sir Vulgrin. Though you are inspiration to all of us this day, I do hate to see any man risk himself so. A man of your bravery is too valuable to us all to throw away in the fetching of a brace of infidel bodies!"

Vulgrin only looked embarrassed. He was in an unusual position, one that few men had occupied: he was looking *down* into the clear blue eyes of Richard of England and Normandy, Aquitaine and Poitou. Perhaps he did not even think about that, that on his destrier he unseemly loomed over and looked down upon a king who was also respected and the captain-general of the crusade. He did see that despite his words, Richard's eyes showed twinkle and his forehead was not creased in a frown.

"It was just the sort of thing my lord king does, sire. Peradventure I did it lest you might, for all Christendom could not afford the throwing away of your life on such as these two infidels."

Richard raised his brows. "Why, you have been trained at court, haven't you! What a fine speech to make, you disrespectful scoundrel!" And he grinned broadly.

Vulgrin looked even more embarrassed. "Please—I apologize . . ."

"Methinks you should have both proper caparison, and banner, and a proper coat of coifed mail, Sir Vulgrin," the king interrupted. "You will not object to my ordering both made for you. These hangers-on that trail us all over this land and slow us so much, must have something to do."

The knight of Montmirail looked stricken. "M-my lord king. I—I c—"

"Cannot afford either," Richard guessed, speaking very quietly. "I can, and you have done me and us all service this day. You will accept these things as gifts of these hands—unless you consider yourself too loyal a subject of King Philip to accept aught from his beloved cousin!" He chuckled. "No no, do not make reply, lad—I see that I embarrass you. Accept thanks, and send your squire to me with drawings and measurements." Suddenly he pointed a finger as if in warning. "Before sunset, Sir hero!"

"Oh, sire—"

"You might also bid him pluck a few of those arrows out of your mail, before their weight unhorses you!" Richard stepped back two paces and raised a hand in salutation. "Well done," he boomed, "Sir Vulgrin of Montmirail!" And, to make the youthful knight less uncomfortable, he turned away. "These corpses will rejoin their comrades, but not until the morrow. Dump them over there somewhere."

He pointed, and two men hurried to obey.

Trying not to look at the many, many friendly grins, Vulgrin paced his horse through the host, back toward the banners of France and his own tent. For it was one of the several problems of this crusade, and the worst: they were not in truth an army. The French remained together and vied with the English and Germans and Austrians and Italians, all of whom they saw as rivals, and the Italians, Austrians, Germans and English did the same. Their kings and archdukes and even churchmen frequently disagreed as to tactics and goals and spoils, even as to the location of sleeping areas. The nearest thing to a common language among them was Latin, and certainly not all men spoke or understood it, even the words of the liturgy they heard during mass.

Just now, however, a knight of France had performed a valiant and dramatic deed, and been personally thanked and saluted by the king of the English. Just now, all the men of the Christian host were united—saving only those who could look upon such an act as Vulgrin's with mean-spirited envy. They stood in their steel-clad thousands and their many colors under their nobles' banners of many hues, and gazed smiling upon young Sir Vulgrin of Montmirail in Frankland.

"*In addition to this direct assault the mangonel could also be used to bombard the interior of the place, the huge stones smashing the buildings beneath and causing casualties. To promote disease and despondency within the walls, it was common practice to launch dead animals, corpses and even prisoners across the wall from the mangonel.*"

—IAN HOGG, "SIEGE TECHNIQUES" in H. W. Koch's *Medieval Warfare*, 1978

SEVEN

The Spy

The Christian camp awoke next day to grisly horror. The gray-faced squire to an English knight stammered the dreadsome news, and soon word was all over the sprawling encampment. During the night, one or more Saracen spies had dared creep in among their sleeping enemies. Not only had he or they made their way safely out again, they had taken a trophy: the head of Sir Reginald of Cumberland. It had been sliced off while that good English knight slept so that his tent was floored with dark coagulated blood.

None of the usually contentious barons made any objection at all when their royal leader demanded that tonight each must contribute one additional man as all-night sentry. They all showed delight at the order of an archery barrage, too, and were pleased to order out men to aid in bringing up more great stones for Pretty Girl and smaller ones for the catapults. Their only grumbling this day was at Henry of Champagne and Hugh of Burgundy, who still had not arrived with their combined force.

By noon, four catapults had sent thirty-eight smallish stones flying over the wall and into Darum. It was just at noon that the Frankish Captain-general had planned the ghastly and demoralizing shock for his enemies in the town. Meanwhile, the troublesome bombardment by arrows and catapults.

Catapults were smallish weapons operating on the same principle as the crossbow, though hardly as portable. While usually provided with larger crews, they could be loaded, wound, and triggered by one man. The framework was less than six feet tall but afforded some protection for that man. Richard and the other nobles saw to it that each of the little siege engines was further protected by at least four archers, each with a long portable shield. That did not stop the occasional catapultier or bowman from being struck by an arrow or missile catapulted from within the fortress.

As ever on the field of battle, priests, leeches and nurses remained busy.

It was from the mangonel that the cruel surprise for the Saracens would come, at high noon. King Richard's engineer Christian presided over that engine, and he had aimed and calculated with care. Now he was sure that Pretty Girl's missiles would clear the wall, rather than slam into it.

A long-faced man reputedly covered with hair despite its sparseness on his head, Christian had been with the master of Normandy for years. He had long ago merited a good coat of chain, a gift of his lord. His over-tunics, of the dull dust color he preferred, were bordered in scarlet. He wore no beard and, laboriously, shaved almost every day with his fine dagger. Another gift from Richard, it followed the successful siege of Taillebourg, on the bank of the Charente in Poitou.

That victory Christian had helped Richard win when the latter was only six months past his twenty-first birthday, back in '79. Christian had been 26, and competent, and nearly as impressive as the young "general" Richard, who had taken his first castle at age 18. Now Christian was 39, twice wounded, often cursed and railed at by his ever-impatient lord, and yet more honored than many nobles. Indeed, Richard often styled him a noble—if "Sir Mangonel" might be considered a worthy title.

As the vicious sun of Palestine approached its zenith in a sky the color of a pot of molten copper, Christian supervised the winding of the windlass that brought down Pretty Girl's great missile-cup.

"Ready for loading, sire," Sir Mangonel said, with a fond pat of the gigantic siege engine with the improbable name.

"Load," Richard the King said, without taking his staring gaze off the lofty wall of Darum.

Christian stood back while two men-at-arms tucked their odious burden into the mangonel's cup-like sling. They stepped out of the way to enable Christian to inspect the positioning of that missile. Hands on hips, he paced around the huge cup, making faces the while. He muttered something, solely to himself. At last he glanced at the two men, and nodded.

"Ready for launching, sire."

Richard glanced at Robert of Dreux, at Guillaume or William of Caieux in his dragon-topped helm. Both barons stood staring at him, neither caring to look again into the mangonel's cup and its contents. Their liege-lord nodded.

"Stand by to reload. Stand by to release." He whirled. "Trumpeters! *Nowww!*" And, to Christian and his assistants: "As the trumpet blasts wane."

Trumpets were simple and ancient. The Romans had possessed and blown them and other horns, time out of mind. The Turks had theirs. They had learned that under this leader, Malek Rik, the Franks used trumpet-signals as commands; Charge, Retreat, Stand Fast. The information did them little good, since Richard changed the signals consistently. This time he wanted the blaring note of six of the horns, sounded simultaneously, only as drama. Let the Turks wonder for a moment or two—and then they would receive his gift.

The six men stood erect, put instruments to lips and sucked up great breaths, and their leader slapped his leather-clad leg in signal. Almost together, they blew. At once the six notes joined as one, a brassy blasting call that peeled out across the plain, echoed off the walls of Darum and the westward hill, rose into the brassy sky. Within the fortressed town, dark-faced sons of Allah glanced at each other and hurried to stare, to try to learn what was signaled; what was coming. The voice that snapped "Now" was unheard save by the men close to the mangonel . . .

With a great whistling rush and a *whump!* the long pole rushed upward to slam against its stay. The cup disgorged its missile and thousands of eyes watched it hurtle through the air, arcing, obviously to clear the stone wall of Darum.

It did not twist and roll ponderously and yet almost gracefully in air, like a stone, for it was not a stone. It had no grace in its flight, this missile. Its arms and legs flailed loosely as it cleared the wall and descended to splatter horribly into the town below. To all who saw from within, it was horror; to anyone it chanced to hit or even land close beside, it was worse than horror.

A good hit by a stone from this same mangonel had knocked him off the wall; an impetuous dash and the hooks of a grapnel had fetched him from the base of that wall; a single ax-stroke had this morning removed his head; and now Pretty Girl hurled back into Darum the blood-blackened corpse of a fellow Saracen slain on yester day, a headless archer.

The great cry that rose from the defenders was audible to the besieging Franks, and not all of them grinned or laughed and cheered. They too understood that horror, and some were unable to exult at such hideous treatment of the dead, even a Christless Saracen.

"Loaded and ready to launch, sire."

Richard stood staring at the wall that denied him access to another conquest. His fingers were moving, counting seconds without his conscious knowledge. "A moment more, Christian. Let them gather around the body, wailing, cursing us . . . while others come hurrying up . . . now they mutter,

122

and seek to determine which man we have so thoughtfully returned . . . *Now!*"

And the second headless Saracen went flying through the still air of noon to slam down among his living fellows.

Richard nodded. "We'll give the whoresons the heads of those two in the morning. Until then, be sure to keep them in sacks lest none of us can bear the stench by eventide!"

Snowy surcoat flapping about his linked mail, he strode away, to order a mock charge in hopes of enticing the angry Turks out to fight in the open.

They did not sally forth. Instead, one of their engines within the town returned the head of Reginald of Cumberland.

That afternoon Guy of Messaria visited with an old friend, and that night he acceded to the Austrian knight's request: he introduced him to Sir Vulgrin of Montmirail.

"Well met, Sir Knight," Guy's battlefield friend Geldemar of Wertheim said, in fair French. He had doffed mailed leggings and surcoat and oddly, wore a singlet in his colors over his chaincoat.

Vulgrin blinked, but took the proffered hand. Soon, over a bit of wine in the blue and white tent of the foreigner, a landless son of a foreign baron and a minor lady-in-waiting, the young Frenchman was confessing that he had never even met an Austrian before and had not expected to take the hand of one, or to share wine and conversation.

"We are all one in God's holy work," Geldemar said in the sententious way of a priest, and Vulgrin looked a bit nonplussed while Guy Kingsaver grinned. All three men had eased off their broad weapons belts to sit or sprawl here in Geldemar's tent, which was far from over-large.

"I'd wager you knew not even where the isle of Cyprus was," the big Austrian said. "Certainly I did not, afore I met Guy."

"Still is," Guy said, peering into his wine-cup. He had hours ago removed chaincoat and wore leather leggings and jerkin over a full-sleeved white tunic or shirt.

Geldemar's thick brows drew down as the other young man stared at him. "What?"

"You said 'where Cyprus was' and I remind you that it still is."

Geldemar smiled. "Oh." He laughed.

Vulgrin swirled the wine in his cup, drank. "I, ah, admit to it: I still know not where lies our friend Guy's home." He gestured. "Just names. Cyprus, Austria, Poitou, Boulogne, Wertheim..."

"*Vert-hyeemmm*," Geldemar said, pronouncing exaggeratedly for the Frank's edification. "Me, I can place Frankland on a map, and Normandy, and Rome, too. Montmirail—nay. Angle-land...*England*...I am none so sure about. On the other hand, who ever heard of Darum?"

"Who ever cared?"

"Who cares *now?*"

The three laughed together. As they subsided, Vulgrin said, "Saladin cares!" so that they all laughed again. As they were starting to sober this time, Guy spoke.

"In the sea. The Mediterranean." He gestured. "Out there."

The fully mailed Vulgrin glanced that way and of course saw only the inner wall of Geldemar's tent. He looked away from the braided belt the Austrian had taken off a Saracen he had slain. "What? In the sea? What?"

"Cyprus," Guy said, and all three laughed as if it were the hilarious jest of a superb minstrel. All jests and japes became so, when war filled young men with tension they needed to release.

"I suppose everyone knows where Frankland is," Vulgrin said.

Guy said "What? Frank what?" while Geldemar was saying, "Ah, but what of Montmirail? Think you it be closer to Wertheim or Lutetia?"

He and Vulgrin chuckled and reached for more wine; Guy looked puzzled.

"What? Lu-teats-what?"

"Lutetia," Vulgrin said, twisting in an attempt to scratch under his mailcoat. "The old Roman name for Paris. The Romans founded it. Julius, I think. It too is on an island, you know."

"Rome?"

"No, Paris, you son of a camel!"

"Ha! Son of camel is it, you son of a defrocked priest and an amorous French pastry!"

"Son of a Cyprian plough-horse and a, uh, yellow kitty-cat!"

"Careful," Geldemar said, smiling. "I am a bastard, you know."

Vulgrin looked at him. "Really? By birth?"

"Of *course*, by birth. By nature I am a passing sweet fellow." With that the Austrian collapsed laughing.

Guy fell back chuckling.

"What? You laugh?" Geldemar demanded, then looked pained. "Son of whomever and a whatever-it-is, I must go and answer a call of nature." He stood up.

"I understand," Guy said, suddenly straight-faced. "It is the lack of women out here. I too am randy—though I do not tell everyone when I sneak off to give myself release!" He held up his right hand, regarded it fondly. "Ah, my dear, my dear!"

Vulgrin looked shocked at first, for all this frank japery was new to him and bordered on the sacrilegious. Yet he was learning, and no longer a squire and a boy, and he made his try at being one with this dangerously naughty pair: "You'll go blind!"

Geldemar the Landless fell down laughing.

Geldemar returned from emptying his bladder to find Vulgrin on his feet, completing the buckling of his weapons belt about his lean hips.

"What's this? Going so soon and us only just met? Why man there is wine left to drink and lies still to be told! Guy and I have not even told you how we came to meet!"

That held Vulgrin awhile; interrupting each other, Guy and Geldemar told the recently knighted Frank of the siege of Acre a year ago, and of the illness that struck so many, including both kings: Philip and Richard. The latter felt that he must show his own men as well as the Saracen that he was not indisposed in his pavilion, but prove to them not only that he was well, but that he was a super-man. Accordingly one day he bade Guy don his armor and mount his destrier, Fauvel. That Guy did, bearing the lion-heart's lance with its scarlet pennon and three grinning leopards. As ordered, he paraded, invisible within a head-compassing helmet, through the crusader encampment and then out, before the walls of Acre.

Only one other man was armored and ahorse among the Christians that morning: Geldemar. And that was the morning on which the defenders of Acre decided upon a sortie!

The great gate swung open. Cymbals clashing and horns blaring, out charged the Saracen knights, fifty strong—and for some mad reason or lack of reason Geldemar charged them: one against fifty! Equally madly, Guy Kingsaver gave Fauvel his rein. That noble warhorse naturally galloped after Geldemar's big black mount.

The leader of the Turks made a mistake, and/or his horse did, and in moments all fifty were streaming back into their city, chased by two mailed knights of Christendom, pennons streaming—one of whom was not even a knight and was for the first time wearing full armor!

"The hard part," Geldemar told the open-mouthed Vulgrin, "was gaining this great fool's attention and getting him to break off the chase, else he'd have galloped right into Acre and doubtless been cut to pieces!—or worse, suppose he had subdued the whole city alone and brought disgrace on all the rest of us!"

Guy was chuckling. "We fled back, with arrows about us thicker than flies in the outhouse. And know you what my lord Richard's words to me were, shouted far more loudly than any deathly ill man should have been able? *'Damn your beardless chin, if there's a scratch on that horse I'll have your head on a trencher!'* "

"This cannot be true!" Vulgrin said. "Surely you—they fled?"

"Aye, but was not in fear, surely," a suddenly sober Guy told him. "They are not so cowardly, these Saracen. Make no mistake about that, Vulgrin, and do not fail to respect their valor and their dangerousness. Even their women fight, as I learned the day we at last broke into Acre!" *Ah, Leila,* he thought, *Leila who first attacked me and, once subdued, loved me so well!*

"Ah, but that is another story of your constant good fortune and constant fuckery," Geldemar said. "How we were rewarded, Vulgrin, for our accidental heroism!"

Vulgrin nodded. "I can imagine. I had evidence on yesterday of the generosity of the Duke of Normandy."

"We were given this geegaw and that," Guy put in, "and . . . two women. Girls! Attractive girls, even—for us, a gift of that same Duke of Normandy, not to mention King of England—and lord of Cyprus!"

Vulgrin stared, mouth open. Guy and Geldemar nodded solemnly and both swore just as solemnly. Vulgrin swallowed. Geldemar heaved a great sigh.

"Eva and Constance," he said with a reminiscent smile. "Blond as buttercups, both of them. Since we could not decide which was whose, we each had each. Ach, Gott, what a night that was, eh Guy?"

Guy sighed and nodded. "Aye. What a night. And it was *Ida* and Constance, gelded-mar, not Eva! Yet I can understand your forgetting—I am not sure that either of us has so much as set eyes upon a woman since."

"Seems that way," Geldemar said, although that night a year ago had not been the last time these two had run upon sexual adventures, and shared women. Then he aborted his morose look to clap the Frank's mailed shoulder and say, "You see, Vulgrin? Ye don't want to be taking leave of us, man—where Guy and I go, adventure appears!"

Vulgrin was still shaking his head, believing the unbelievable because it was so. But he managed a smile as he said, "Oh? Stay with you, is it, when you have just said a year has passed since you have so much as seen a woman! Nay, I must to my own tent, and to bed, ere I fall asleep while I stand here."

They could not dissuade him, and he departed.

Geldemar dropped the tent's flap and dropped into his sleeping mat. "Good fellow," he said. "May well be innocent—I think me we may have done embarrassment on him! Just a boy, isn't he?"

"Aye—but have care now—it might take me months to raise a beard."

"Not what I meant," Geldemar assured him. "Nay, Guy, nay. In experience, I mean. In knowledge, in war and loving . . . methinks yon Vulgrin has much and much yet to learn. Only a month since his knighting!" He shook his head. "And probably too brave for his own good."

"Ha! That from the maniac who charged fifty Saracen so that I dared do nothing but follow and try to pull you out! Well now—do not be quaffing the last of that wine, my friend, for now the call of nature has come upon me."

"The what?"

"I have to piss," Guy said, and rose with a rustle of leathern leggings.

"Better take your pretty sticker," Geldemar said, indicating Guy's dagger. Like his sword, it was sheathed and attached to the belt lying beside the other man's.

"I want to drain it," Guy said, "not cut it off!"

While his Austrian comrade chuckled, he departed the tent into the moonless night of Palestine.

The stars were there in their myriads, clear and cold and bright, so that he was just able to see. He decided to betake himself a little away from Geldemar's tent; it was hardly a friendly act to give it the odor of souring urine. With reinforcements failing to come, this damned siege might drag on for weeks!

Quietly he stepped behind a big tent whose color he could not be sure of, in the wan starlight. He had just finished watering the ground and was fastening his leggings when he heard the odd little scrabbling sounds from a few feet away.

A rat, he thought, and wished he had brought his dagger after all—better still, his sword! He glanced around at the ground, squinting in his effort to see. He spotted a roundish stone only a little bigger than his fist. Even more quietly now, he squatted to pick it up. Then he peeped around the corner of the tent . . . in time to see a hand appear from under the side of a very nearby one. The hand pushed forth a head-sized leathern sack. It was a smallish hand. A *dark* hand.

Guy stood staring, cogitating. A knight had brought some lad into his tent to slake his sexual needs, mayhap, and now sent him away surreptitiously?—with a reward? A dark-complected youth? A Saracen boy?

No, not necessarily; all of us are burned dark of hands and face by this terrible sun that hates us so! Too, some full-grown men had small hands, just as the hands of others

129

were nigh the size of hams from early-killed pigs.

Not necessarily a Saracen, then (and not likely either), he thought as he watched the other hand come out from under the tent. The fingers of both dug in a little to pull their owner out. And not necessarily a lad, either, lean-armed in snug dark sleeves that appeared to be black, at least in the starlight. On the other hand, the means he was using to depart the tent were distinctly unusual, both surreptitious and suspicious. And that bag...

I'm watching the escape of a thief, Guy Kingsaver thought, and his arm tensed, hand tightening on the stone it held. He started to move.

But wait. Suppose it was not a thief, and his first surmise was correct? This fellow must be accosted, but it could be handled quietly. No use making enough noise to rouse others and embarrass the knight within, if he had indeed been engaging in a homosexual act. He was hardly the first to resort to such means, whether it was for the first time in his life or no.

Then the head appeared, and Guy saw the strangeness of a turban black as jet. It covered a dark face to the brows— a dark face with a nose whose end was down-turned a bit as if to keep sand from blowing up the nostrils. Not a European nose. More: this definitely Semitic skulker held a lean, shortish dagger clenched in his teeth. The Crusader swallowed—and twitched his head back out of sight when he saw the other's head start to turn, doubtless to glance this way and that before crawling the rest of the way out and—running off? As thief or sex partner or, considering that dagger, worse?

Guy waited a moment before peering out once more.

Now he saw the skulker halfway out, dressed in snug black, worming with care for silence. The dagger was no longer in his mouth, but Guy saw its faint silvery glint on the ground; the now more-than-suspicious night-skulker

(Turk, or native Palestinian, or Jew, perhaps, though the last was hardly likely) held it in his right hand. With that ringless fist he pushed the sack along the ground before him. His other hand, also without rings, pulled him forward. A black sash appeared and then an unboyishly longish backside. Again: snugly black-clad.

I may have to apologize to someone for this, the Crusader thought, and in four swift steps he had a booted foot planted on the wrist of the knife-hand. He had not stamped, but merely stepped down to immobilize that hand. A dark face jerked up at him as he heard a grunt of surprise and pain, and eyes stared. Their sclera were exaggeratedly white in the night and against a face Guy now felt sure had been deliberately darkened.

Then the other hand moved, jerking over to grasp the bag and slam it against Guy's ankle. It was his turn to grunt in pain, boots or not; the sack contained what felt like a large round stone. Had this thief perhaps stolen some knight's helmet?

He lost his balance and had to step back. Instantly the hand with the dagger moved, blade flashing in a streak, and Guy had to jerk his foot back another pace to avoid being stabbed through the foot. The other came out of the tent fast now, almost in silence, using the sack-hand to push himself to his feet—and the Crusader pounced to that side, away from the dagger-hand, and struck with the stone.

It seemed to *sink into* the turbanned head, and Guy felt gooseflesh at the strangeness of that sensation. The face went straight down into the ground, even as the knife-hand swung at him. Guy avoided it, flipping his stone into his left hand while he swung a leg across the prostrate fellow's back. Bestriding it, he sat swiftly. As he did so his right hand leaped down to grasp the wrist of the dagger-hand. He felt a leather bracer under the snug black cloth, and a lean wrist.

Both strugglers maintained the silence they had broken only by grunts of pain.

Now the other hand was swinging the sack back, the thief blindly trying to strike his assailant. Automatically and almost as blindly Guy struck it away with the stone in his left hand, while his right hung onto the wrist of the deadly hand. The fist-sized stone made a cracking sound against the underside of the forearm, and this time the prostrate thief's grunt was mingled with a little cry he tried to bite off, a high-pitched sound of real pain. Those dark fingers twitched reflexively open and the sack they had been swinging leaped away as if propelled. It hit the ground with a solid yet dull and almost mushy sound, and popped open. Out rolled its contents.

It was not a stone.

Guy of Messaria stared at it as it rolled awkwardly: the gory, severed head of someone he did not know. A knight, judging from the short hair whacked off the better to fit within a coif. The poor fellow must have been sleeping, for the eyes were closed in the way of no one freshly beheaded. Murdered as he slept then, not slain in any sort of struggle. And this man had been alive only minutes ago; the blood at the neck was still wet. It smeared the sandy earth.

It's no mere thief I have caught, but the fiend who creeps into our camp by night to murder! Last night he slew Sir Reginald of Cumberland and tonight—this poor wight who never knew what befell him!

With that thought Guy gasped out a snarling sound and swung his stone viciously in at the side of his captive's turbanned head. But the smallish fellow was moving, twisting like an eel, and again the turban absorbed most of the impact. The murderer emitted only an "uh" sound, still twisting, and then was on his back and staring up at his captor, right arm straining hard to swing the dagger. Guy held it down, and when he started again to swing his stone his own wrist was caught. So they struggled in the darkness, in silence, and the Cypriot never knew why he did not shout an alarm or a loud *"Au succors!"*—"help!"

Then footsteps came, and Geldemar was hurrying up.

"Wondered what was keeping y—*Gott!*" he snapped, and in reflex at seeing the newly severed head, he kicked the dagger-hand viciously.

The knife spun away. The Austrian's big hand closed on the captive's head and yanked. The turban came away in its many folds—and a goodly mass of glossy hair spilled out, black as night. All three of them gasped, and suddenly Guy Kingsaver released the stone, yanking back his hand, and slammed it down onto the killer's chest.

He felt the upthrusting protrusion, and knew that this was no boy they had caught, and indeed no male of any sort.

"A girl!" he gasped.

Eight

A Murderer Pays

Smiling grimly, Geldemar stood watching Guy fuck the murdering Saracen witch. The Austrian was unconscious that his hand was at his crotch, massagingly idly while he waited to take his turn. He watched his friend's tight small butt bounce up and down, cheeks clamping to drive him into the murdering Saracen. Geldemar could see that the other man was using his cock as a bludgeon that inwardly battered the bitch. Good! The head of a knight of Christendom was not all she'd had in that leathern bag. The slender monster had also severed his penis with her razor-edged blade. She had meant to carry it, too, back into Darum.

Now she moaned and groaned, reduced to a cock-housing well as that long Cypriot cock ripped in and out of her battered vagina and widened the whole steaming chamber. Geldemar saw a shiver tear through her when Guy's hands slid under to cup her silken haunches.

Good, Geldemar thought. *Give the murderous beast every inch of it and make a new hole in there!*

Clutching her smallish bottom with both hands and scooping her up, Guy forced her jet-furred loins hard against his to be sure her murderer's cunt was opened wide—and deeply pierced. Grinding, he hammered his inflated, swollen prick into the warm layered folds of her slippery cleft, fucking her with pile-driving thrusts. He saw the shiver that curveted through her at the feel of her prostrate form being opened further and deeper by his stiff stalk.

His breath blew hot over her face as he humped her hard in a lewd undisguised lust and desire to punish.

She quivered in horror and humiliation, caught and gagged and tied ignominiously to be raped by two Franks. He who had discovered and in truth overpowered her was using her now, but she knew that he was only *first;* the thicker man was only waiting his turn to rut in her. She had not thought it would be like this. She had not thought she would be caught at all. She could not afford to think about that possibility; she was so full of hate and the rewards were so great. How they admired and hailed her, in the city—a woman! But now...

Terribly aware of the distention of her strained and quivering legs, she also felt some pain. Already her widely stretched lower lips were sore. What a cock this big awful Frank's false god had awarded him, rot his eyes and soul! The thick and lengthy thing was like a bludgeon bashing around inside her, banging and battering her cunt's delicate tissues.

She was opened wide, wider than she had ever been, feeling terribly stretched and stuffed as he ground in and his bulbous-headed organ flailed in and out of her tortured canal. She groaned, clenching her teeth, and tried to think herself far from here.

That was not possible. She could not prevent her reactions. She moaned and shivered each time his big swollen penis shoved so far into her. His rutting lunges drove it hard and long between the resilient lobes that puffed at the base of her quivering belly to frame the chamber of hot flesh. This accursèd Frank seemed bent on turning it into a cavern her Afdal would spurn; a cavern fit for the immense prong of a rutting horse.

Thick his *zubb* was, like a quarterstaff in her, like one of their broad Nazareni swords, like a tent-pole. Tears filled her eyes, not from the pain of it but at thought of what he was doing to her vagina; the channel that Afdal loved so well. *Had* loved so well.

Like grimly tolling bells his hairy bollocks thumped the delicate furrow just below her stuffed and widened cunt. In and out he pounded, out of control. The need was on him. It had been on him before he left the tent, with his and Geldemar's talk of the past and his own thought reminding him of sex, of women, of fucking. And then the adrenaline surge when he had seen the skulker, all lean and black-clad, and the struggle in the dark . . . and then revelation upon revelation. First, that the supposed thief was a spy and a murderer, the killer of Sir Reginald and now of another crusading knight . . . and then that the captive killer was female! A girl of the enemy, and not one who fought on the battlefield, but who skulked in snug black cotton and murdered sleeping men that their heads might be catapulted back among their fellows.

Her mouth was gagged with her own turban, a great wad of black silk that propped her jaws wide while rendering her almost incapable of sound. Rolled shreds of her garments bound her wrists tightly behind her—under her, now. The long, long strip of dark blue cloth with which she had wound and bound her wideset young breasts bound her ankles far apart—to Geldemar's sword-scabbard, which was a yard long. Naked, pretty breasts jiggling, she lay on the floor of Geldemar's tent and took Guy's anger and his arousal.

He strained in, felt the thick hot shaft sink deliciously deep, again and again, to the deeps of her Saracen belly. She was so hot and snug inside that he groaned. Then he shuddered throughout his long body, and with a series of gasps he jetted his sperm into her, to her very depths.

He collapsed on her, huffing and making her squirm under the dead weight of his spent body.

After a few moments he heard the voice from behind and

above: "Uh, old friend . . . you are not alone here, you know."

With a sigh, Guy pushed himself up onto his palms. He stared down at her, his shrinking cock still contained within her inundated cunt. Her eyes were bright, deep brown, sparkling and alive with hate. He saw the hatred that had led her to uncommon bravery in entering this camp, and yet to acts of base cowardice: the murder of sleeping men. For an instant her face was replaced by a vision: the face of the knight she had so recently slain. With a sound that was almost a snarl. Guy slammed in his hips, goring into her one last time.

Then he left her naked, bound body with a jerk, *yanking* his dripping cock out of her distended slit. He saw her quaking jerk of reaction to the pain of swift withdrawal, and he nodded grimly. *Good.*

He glanced at his friend, then blinked and stared.

Geldemar grinned. He wore his leggings, tapes undone so that they were open only at the crotch—and he had pulled on his mailcoat.

"You—you're . . .?"

Geldemar nodded. "Aye. I am going to fuck the naked bitch while wearing my mail. She is a killer; good chainmail should feel good against her naked skin. Oh—and may I rot if I follow that tent-pole of yours up her cunt, Guy. Nay, it is the garden gate I shall breech. Surely she has reserved back there a nice tight hole for my cock. Help me turn her before I burst, will you?"

She tried to fight, to struggle, throwing herself this way and that in such a way that she must have understood what Geldemar intended.

That availed her nothing, of course. He grasped each of her breasts and twisted, then slapped both. He flipped her over onto them, onto her belly, her legs twisting as the sword scabbard came up and over with a clatter. He began loosing her ankles from it, then. When he had the right free, she kicked blindly, face down, and caught the squatting Austrian in the thigh so that he was tumbled backward. He rose and grasped his sword.

"Mar!"

"Oh be not silly, Guy. I've no intention of slaying the bitch while I still have this erection up to my navel! And he brought the flat of his sword down across both her upturned buttocks, with strength.

The blow was hard, and its impact was loud in the containing tent. Guy saw the sword actually sink in a little, so hard had Geldemar struck. For an instant she was still and silent, her pubis slammed into the floor of his tent and her rearward cheeks partially flattened by the wide and shining blade. Then she came alive. Wretched sounds of pain emerged through her jaws-propping gag and the muscles of her arms stood out in her attempts to drag them free of their bondage. Her unbound leg flailed wildly. But she was struggling fruitlessly and kicking blindly, face down with her wrists bound just above her darkly striped arsecheeks.

Geldemar caught her flying ankle, pressed it, said "Be still," and released her. The foot flailed. With a shake of his head, he brought his sword down onto her butt again, severely flattening and darkening those resilient cheeks. Once her shivers and wild response slackened, he again pressed his hand firmly onto her right ankle.

Again he said "Be still."

Both men heard the sound of a sob and saw the quake of it take her body. They also saw her drop her foot to the floor and lie still while Geldemar freed her other foot of his scabbard. Rising from her, he went to the small barrel or keg in the corner of the tent; it was about a third of the size of a standard rain-barrel. He rolled it over to the prostrate girl and positioned it as and where he wanted it, on its side. After bracing it with helmet and scabbard, he hoisted the prone girl.

Rather than arrange her across the keg, he dumped her there. Shudders took her as her breasts and bare belly were abraded by the rough old wood. Her arms had to be monstrously uncomfortable tied so in the small of her back, with her over the keg, head down. Her feet dragged the floor on this side, so that her rump was thrust high, its cheeks parted despite her obvious attempts to clench them.

To the staring Guy, it seemed that those twice-struck buttocks actually glowed. He could see the swelling of the two lurid welts Geldemar's sword had put there. Guy was not sure that he'd have been able to treat even this beast so brutally—but he was glad Geldemar had.

But to fuck even such a murdering monster, her naked with me in mail—that I'd not be able to do, he mused. *Surely 'tis a shamefully unmanly weakness in me, this love for women and concern for them!*

"If the keg tries to roll," Geldemar said, "I hope I have some friend nearby who will set a foot against it."

Guy nodded. His gaze was on the proferred female rump and the black-furred bulge just below its parted crack, rather than on the luridly red male erection throbbing high just behind it. Geldemar took it in hand, while planting his other hand on the bowed, helpless girl's upturned arse.

He surprised her and Guy both; lowering his aim, he shoved straight into the open, oozing gap his friend had just plumbed.

His cock plunged in easily, furling her labia inward, and slid up a slithery canal made slick by the other man's semen. Guy heard him groan aloud in potent sexual tension, saw his nostrils flare open. Then he saw the other man's lower body hunch in strongly in an attempt to impale her womb—and the keg rolled.

"*Scheiss,*" Geldemar grunted.

Guy said it in French: "*Merde.*"

With a sigh and a shrug he hurried around the little barrel, carrying his leggings. Dropping them on the floor before the girl's hanging head, he plopped his bare butt down on the leggings. Two big hands reached in under her down-streaming hair and closed on her breasts, each about the size of one of her fists. His fingers dug in and a new tremor flowed through her. He extended his legs, bent his knees, and set his heels against either end of the keg. Her gagged face brushed his somnolent crotch.

He looked up into the eyes of his Austrian friend. "Now, Mar."

"Ach, what a friend!" And Geldemar, grinning, gored in strongly while Guy held the keg in place with his feet and the girl in place with both hands biting into her breasts. Geldemar pumped several times.

Then he pulled his cock out of her flooded vaginal gap and shoved it between the striped moons of her arse. The semen-coated head plunged all the way inside the muscular ring of her anus.

For a moment she was quite still, as if she hadn't noticed the swift entry into the extreme constricting tightness of her firmly-muscled young arsehole. Then she made all the noise she could through her mouth's silken stuffing and jerked as if trying to ram her head straight through Guy's belly.

"Hold her!" Geldemar cried, almost desperately.

"She . . . goes . . . nowhere," Guy said.

The Saracen's attempt at a scream of rearward pain curdled in her throat; his powerful hands crushed her breasts too tightly and agonizingly for her to cry out, gag or no gag.

Fighting the tight-clenched, rubbery vise of her sphincter all the way, Geldemar forced his inflexible prick up her virgin rectum. It seemed to grasp him like a hot hand, actually hurting. He gritted his teeth against a groan he did not want the others to hear.

* * *

He was clever enough to hold it there awhile, knowing that no matter what she did, the grip of her protesting hole would slacken and the pain of his invading rod of flesh would become steadily less fiery. He knew, too, that no matter how enraged and outraged she was, if this were any sort of woman at all the pain would slowly meld into an inextricable marriage with pleasure.

He would not wait for that, however, not with this murdering monster. His plan did not call for her liking her embuggerment or even accepting it. She had no more choice than the men she had murdered.

Still ... how delicious to demean her by seeing if he couldn't just *make* this captive killer respond!

Wrapping his hands around her hips, he began running his fingers up and down the widened furrow of her vulva. His fingers sloshed through the semen of his friend, smeared it up over the top of her slit and onto her lower belly. He matted her thick black pubic hair with it, sought out her clitoris and coated it, too. She felt that, right enough; inner muscles twitched in little spasms around the sensitive knob of his cock.

Guy felt a sudden flood of air over his lower belly, just at the base of his penis, and knew she had sighed. With a glance up at the other man, he eased his twin grip and began fondling her raisin-like nipples. She trembled and moaned when the man behind her slid his accursèd uncircumcised prick out until her anal band housed only its swollen head, sighed again when he strained once more to toy with her hot, open-gaping sheath and run a fingertip over her clitoris. A shiver leaped through her at that intimate touch to the area of her highest pleasure. Her anular ring clamped hard and he swallowed, looking surprised. He challenged that grip, pushing.

Again he sank his prick into the hot buttery feel of her rectum, and again he paused to soothe her twitching, slowly erecting clitoris. Her squirming made him smile. Though Guy was younger, strangely enough it had been he who told Geldemar about this little bud of a woman's sensual feeling.

The Cypriot had been taught a very great deal by that Frankish whore Luisa-de-Something, Geldemar knew, and had learned more since by doing, and from other women simply because he was interested and not afraid to learn from them. A strange young man, this hero from Cyprian Messaria! He simply was not one with the rapacious raping barbarians from France and Normandy and England and Italy. (Geldemar knew that Austrians, of course, were *civilized*.)

Again he withdrew his tumid shaft, and again he held it just inside her anal mouth while he slithered his fingers down between her puffy, reddened lower lips. He drew them up, sperm-smeared, to caress what he thought of as her cock-imitator. Guy was doing his part and enjoying it; his big fingers had gone gentle on her dangling titties, smoothing, soothing, pressing their deeply colored raisin tips, caressing them and gently drawing the nipples out and downward.

Those nipples lengthened. The girl squirmed and trembled through her whole length. Her clitoral bud rose. Possessive male hands on her felt her quaking, her tremulous shivers. From behind her, one man winked at another.

Actually straining to reach around while continuing to move his pelvis, Geldemar began moving his slick hard tool in and out of the grippingly slender track of her rectum. The light-clenched band of her sphincter ani clung. The skin of that fleshy ring was stretched so tightly over the flesh that his imbedded shaft seemed about to break it open. His fingers grew busier on her clitoris and Guy's drew, tugging at her nipples while he petted the entire rounded surfaces of her down-swinging tits.

Geldemar groaned aloud. The hot, humid walls of her

narrow rearward entry were flowering in conquered acceptance. Yet still he felt the plastic inner flesh, soft as wet silk, still stretching and yielding and seeming to squirm around the hot bar of flesh buried deeper and deeper up her fundus. The pounding of his racing blood through his cock was a strong erotic beat that she must surely feel, up inside her bowels. He ground against the very firm melons of her upturned arse, boring up the snug hole between them.

Smoother and smoother, easier and easier became the passage of his gliding penis in and out of the gasping girl's relaxing arsehole. She lay helplessly over the barrel, hurting her stomach while he raped her ass . . . and yet four hands and twenty fingers were coaxing relaxation into her. So was the intimate probing of strangely unrapacious cock up her virginal anus.

The victim now shivered constantly, squirmed her hips, and made distinctly un-victimlike noises. Little moaning sighs escaped her gag, and they were not of pain or horror. Quivers ran through and through her bowed form, and they were not of fear. Little warm tingles whipped about in her vagina and through her hanging, fondled tits and into her belly, and they were not of pain or horror or fear. Her nipples grew and her clitoris swelled.

The clever manipulations of that twig combined with the stroking squeezing tugging pressures on her nipples and the stoking of her now-relaxed rearward passage to fill her with the widening glow of rapture. It built and built in her.

Without even knowing it, she began to wag the long oval buns of her pierced backside. Her body began moving backward and forward as well as she could, using her toes against the tent's flooring. Thus she was sliding the long, slippery, warm channel of her asshole to and fro along his cock. It was horrible, shaming, monstrously demeaning—and she could not help herself. Her body had taken control. Her body liked this possession.

His hands digging into her rearcheeks, he grunted and thrust in. Prodding prick sawed in and in. Each deep glide was as one more stroke of a poker into her rearward furnace, stoking its inner fires.

They flared, blazed up, and she moaned and jerked out her climax.

She had never known anything like it. The exquisite splendor of her rolling orgasm raised her to heights of sexual satiation that with Afdal she had not dreamed existed. She wanted to shriek out her joy and her release, but could only moan and snort through her nose, with her mouth stuffed with over a yard of black silk.

Laughing aloud then, Geldemar turned her ass into a cunt and fucked it with all his might, jarring and hammering her, slamming in until his surging hips depressed her taut buttocks, until he cried out and tried to skewer in even farther while he spent and spent into the hot tight channel of her bowels.

Perhaps a minute later he said, "She came, Guy. I—we made her climax! I think me we could free her of all bonds now, and she would not seek to leave us!"

Guy stared up at him. He slid a hand up from one breast to her throat, and pushed upward while he spoke.

"This is a killer, Mar. She has killed at least twice . . . and forget not the mutilation of tonight's victim. It is good that you have demeaned her by forcing her to accept buggery and to climax as well. Just do not be starting to think of her as a girl or a woman or even human, Mar. Not this animal. Free her, aye . . . and then you might lose your cock if not your head!"

Her breath cut off by his hand, she was starting to squirm and shudder anew when Geldemar turned his head away. "Aye. It's right you are, by God's wounds. It is easy to forget, when your cock has just spat into a warm snug pudding and you know she liked it! You are right. So. It is

145

not meet for us to kill her, nor is it our place. Shall we take her to my lord Archduke now?"

"You might let me put on my clothing."

Geldemar laughed. "Feel her movement now when I un-socket, all in a . . . *jerk!*"

"Uh! I felt her movement all right," Guy said in a strained voice. "I seem to have raised a new erection, and in jerking she just butted it. She has a head as hard even as yours!"

"Hmp! Slurs on my person while bragging of a new erection, is it? Well, get up man, and slide it into one of these holes—we've well-greased them both!"

"Why give her further pleasure?"

At last Guy released her neck, and she hung limp, her nostrils working like a bellows as she snorted for breath. He rose. "Archduke Leopold? I thought to take her to King Richard."

Geldemar shrugged. "We are in the Austrian section of the camp, and in the tent of an Austrian knight. Well you know how those two get along! My good lord would scream and rail and curse, did we not fetch her to him. Would the Lion-heart?"

"No, but he'd not be happy."

"Umm. Have you ever heard the one about the lesser of two evils?"

Guy nodded, but went past the other man to the tent's flap. He opened it, looked up at the sky.

"Uh," he said, returning for his leggings. "I fear me it be too late to take her to anyone, this night. Methinks we may well be the only men awake! On the morrow, Geldemar, on the morrow." He began pulling on his clothes.

"Oh." Geldemar pointed. "And you walk about wagging your tail in front, and talk of keeping her here, and yet you are not interested in taking the hardness out of that veritable sword sticking out of your crotch?"

"No. I want nothing more to do with her."

146

"Strange fellow! She is a woman with available orifices, and you are a man wearing a poker designed to fill orifices!"

"I am a rutting animal with a hard on, Mar, true. But this be no woman, this is the very worst of our enemies, because the others meet us face to face. No. Admittedly I come late to sense and scruples, but I have said it: I have done with her." Suddenly he turned from clothing himself to look at his friend, eyebrows up. "Still . . . what sort of knight are you, Geldemar, with your squire only a few feet away somewhere, and *that*—he pointed at the girl over the barrel—"here available, as you said, with *available orifices,* and you think not of calling Jordan to let him empty his balls? Hmp!"

Geldemar cocked his head. "Jordan! By the cross, I do become a brainless animal in rut! I had forgot him altogether! O'course! I shall rouse him at once. Do you watch *this* a moment, will you now?"

"Aye. Just beware of running into that special detail who had to go bring in the monster boulders, Mar. They might want to put you to work."

"Work? Ugh!"

Legginged and mailcoated, he was at the tent's entry when he paused, frowning. Then he turned back to take up his weapons belt. He buckled it on without a word, and sheathed his sword. He looked at Guy. Guy nodded. His friend need say nothing. They had caught the beheading night-murderer . . . or one of them. Who could feel quite safe in the darkness outside now, without sword and dagger? With a return nod, Geldemar started out.

"Oh, Sir Hardhead—about your squire Jordan. Has he not friends?"

Geldemar turned back to stare. "No doubt. They may even have friends as well!" He looked past Guy at the upturned bottom of their captive murderer.

"No doubt," Guy said. "And what of the poor men-at-arms of Austria, so long without proper release and their balls doubtless swollen big as their fists, eh?"

Again the Austrian looked at her—at her arse, rather, and the backs of her legs. "Aye," he said quietly, thoughtfully, and he was no longer smiling. "And I shall keep a tally of how many yon bitch . . . entertains, between now and dawn."

Geldemar of Wertheim left the tent, nodding and wearing a grim smile. Guy swung to check the girl's bonds before he too departed her silent company, strapping on his weapons belt. He made his way back toward the squires' tent near Richard's pavilion. He would not disturb the leader, but he had no desire to remain longer in Geldemar's tent. He needed sleep, and had an idea there would be no sleeping in that place, not this night!

Next morning the Archduke of Austria came calling on the Lion-heart. He was a thick burly man with a homely face notable for a broad, thick mustache. The broadness of his shoulders and his massive chest emphasized his short stature. Archduke Leopold ruled Austria, which was sovereign and yet not a kingdom, and acted as if he ruled half of Europe or more. He and Richard had had their troubles, and it had not been too long ago that Richard had so thoroughly lost his temper with Leopold that he had ejected the man from his tent—literally kicking his butt in the process. That could not be forgiven or forgotten, but still the two men were here on holy Crusade, and obliged to conduct business.

Richard ordered his high-and-mightiness admitted to his pavilion at once. Leopold entered as majestically as he could on those short, thick legs. Doubtless he fancied that the tall, nodding plume of red above his helmet made him appear taller. It did not. At two inches above six feet, Richard was not quite a foot taller than his fellow monarch.

"Milord," he said formally, rising at once. Within his

148

own pavilion the size of a large chamber, he wore not the white surcoat with crusader's cross emblem, but a red singlet emblazoned on the chest with his three leopards in gold, and belted in white leather. His head was bare and his sunset hair undressed and indeed tousled.

"Milord," Leopold said just as formally, and remained several feet distant that he need not look up to meet the other man's blue, blue eyes. He was fully armored and wearing a fresh white surcoat bearing the Austrian version of the cross. He wore sword and dagger, but entered alone. Three others were present; Richard's young page and his squires Yves of Anjou and Guy of Messaria.

Richard gestured. "Will you have—

"I will have nothing, my lord Duke." The archduke stood with his spurred feet apart as if bracing an enemy and hooked a thumb into his broad, silver-worked weapons belt. "Know you a knight among my company named Ludovic of Drava Marsh?"

Well, Richard thought at the abruptness of the question and stiffness of its asker, *Lord High-and-Mighty would not have come merely to pass pleasantries, would he!* He said, "Ludovic; Ludvig/Louis. Of *Drahva . . . Marsh?*" He shook his head. "I cannot say that I know either the name or the area, and apologize if I should and my memory needs jogging. What of him?"

"Drava Marsh is in Slovenia, a land just east of Austria. Two Slovenians came hither with me, as did five Hungarians. Sir Ludovic was murdered last night as he lay sleeping. He was beheaded."

"Ah, God!"

"Aye. Further, my knight Geldemar of Wertheim captured the murderer."

"Ah! Now there is a valiant knight I know! And you bring some good tidings at that, then. Where is the whoreson—

I assume it was the same who slew Reginald of Cumberland two nights past?"

"So we assume as well. And it is not a whoreson, this Saracen murderer, but a woman—a mere girl, really."

"Body of Christ!"

"Since Sir Geldemar took her outside the tent of Sir Ludovic, in the Austrian area, he brought her to me. It was very late of the night, and Sir Geldemar had stepped forth to relieve himself. He deemed it too late to waken either of us, but knew who and what he had the moment he saw the contents of the sack of leather she bore. The very head of poor Ludovic, and . . . his privatemost parts."

Richard showed his shock. "Ah, *God!* Satan take all the Saracens! Satan rot the vile wench—and God be thanked that your brave knight captured her! What a reward that good big lad deserves! Where is this monster of a *girl* now?"

Leopold held his straightforward gaze. "Outside, my lord Duke," he said, for he would not use the greater title Richard was entitled to, as monarch of the English. For the matter of that, anyone knew that the Angevin duchy of Normandy with its nice little empire was more important than that foggy little island across the channel—which had after all been conquered by a Norman.

"With Sir Geldemar," Leopold continued, "and the squire of Sir Ludovic, one Valentin of Caranthia—also in Slovenia. I have approved Sir Geldemar's act: he wished not to waken me and yet durst not punish the girl on his own, either. Yet he thought of a way to punish her and provide some recreation as well. I should say that she has been had, roughly of course and both before and behind, by forty or so men: squires and men-at-arms."

Noting that the words "I have approved Sir Geldemar's act" were spoken with a certain truculence, Richard only nodded. This tiny challenge was over a matter of tiny consequence, and so he said, "With my approval as well."

"Since it was my knight she mutilated and murdered most foully, I have had her mutilated in return," Leopold said, just as truculently.

Richard did have to admire the way the man had prepared, and presented one fact at a time, pausing each time to see if trouble were to arise. This last Richard liked not all that much—not that the devil's daughter had been mutilated, but that Lord High-and-Mighty had chosen to do so and *then* bring her to the crusade's acknowledged commander. Nevertheless, was not worth making (more) trouble between him and this haughty, prickly man; and so again he nodded.

The quietly watching Guy Kingsaver could *feel* the tension between these two men. How sad that each had to be the way he was, and that the crusade had to suffer for it!

"She is alive?"

"Of course. And so I have fetched her to the Captain-general of our endeavor. For interrogation, mayhap—she still has a tongue, but speaks only the Paynim language—before the carrying out of punishment on the vile creature. *Further* punishment," he added.

"Umm," the Lion-heart said, nodding still again. "Still has a tongue, eh. And would my good lord of Austria counsel questioning her?"

Leopold blinked in surprise at being asked for advice, and shrugged massive shoulders. "Does it matter what she knows or might tell? If 'twould hasten the fall of Darum, save Christian lives, mayhap . . . "

"My lord Archduke, I doubt not that Darum will be ours on the morrow. Today we do little more than play with them, maintaining the siege—and letting our men rest, to gather their strength and sharpen their weapons for the morrow. Tonight we shall counsel, for I have a plan to present. We are no longer awaiting the French."

"Ah! Without them, Darum shall be *ours*, then."

Richard saw the keenness of the other man's eyes as he

tried to say his words so casually. Both well remembered their trouble after the fall of Acre: whether at the archduke's order or no, some toadspit Austrian soldier had planted the banners of Leopold on high above the fallen city, and it had pleased Richard to climb up himself and remove them. Now the pompous fellow sought to obtain avowal that part of the Saracen town and whatever wealth it contained would belong to him. And Richard might well have promised so—but not to Leopold. Nay, far more amusing to make the strutting cockerel wait and sweat a bit! Peradventure he'd even try to be a decent fellow for the next thirty hours or so!

Let him draw his own conclusions, then; I shall make him no direct answer. "I do thank my lord of Austria, and would like to see your heroic Sir Geldemar and his prize captive. And the good dead knight's squire, if I might."

During all this stiff converse Guy and Yves had said nothing, only exchanging a look and prickling a bit amid the tension. Guy was pleased that he seemed to have had no part in the taking of the prisoner. He needed no more hero's laurels and might well have been railed at or at least chewed on a bit, by Richard, for not having fetched the prisoner here at once.

At the large opening of the huge tent, Leopold turned partway back. "Squire Valentin? May I enquire why you wish to interview him?"

"I said naught of 'interviewing' the lad, my lord. However, he is from a land nigh unknown, and with no countrymen or few among us, and now he is bereft of his lord. How old is he? Think you he is ready for the spurs, or must he be taken in by another?"

Leopold turned fullway around and fixed Richard with his gaze, this time with both thumbs in his broad and shiny weapons belt. Bracing his fellow lord and ruler, with haughty pride.

"My lord of Normandy. I have no notion as to the age of this squire of a knight in my company, who calls me liege-lord. He is a youth. Whether he continues as squire, among my company, or whether *I* choose to knight him— these are concerns of Austria, my lord of Normandy."

"Believe it or no, Austria, I meant no challenge," Richard said mildly, and his eyes were atwinkle even while he thought, *Venal little fart!* He said, "I assure my lord of Austria that I agree: the matter is in his hands. Mayhap I felt that this Valentin of . . . Slovenia might need a bit of friendliness. It is easy to forget that we were once youths ourselves . . . as my good lord forgets that I am Aquitaine and Anjou and Poitou and Aquitaine *and* England, as well as Normandy."

Leopold stared coldly, bobbed his head in a peer's acknowledgment, and swung again to the pavilion's entry. "Sigismund!"

"His squire, sire," Yves Know-naught said quietly, and the king nodded without turning.

They entered with the captive, squire Sigismund and Geldemar and a youth of medium height with darkish skin, wavy brown hair so dark it might as well have been black, and a good nose. He looked more sad than grim.

So did the entirely naked captive, who was hardly able to walk. She hung heavy in the hands that grasped her in the armpits. Her arms were twisted behind her and bound both at wrists and elbows, so that she must jut her chest stiffly and hurtfully despite her obvious weariness. From a leathern cuff about one ankle dragged a chain attached to a water-bag full of stones. They rattled with each tottering step. She was also grimy, bedraggled, one great bruise from neck to knees and particularly in the loins, and bloody of chest and belly.

Mutilation for mutilation, the archduke had said. Aye. Gone were the pretty breasts Guy had handled only a few hours ago, and he looked away. He had to remind himself of what she had done, that he might not think: *Poor girl!*

The thought came anyhow.

He and Geldemar exchanged a look; that was all. Though no one else was looking at him, just now Guy was unable to wink.

She did not have to be thrust to the flooring; when her arms were released, she sagged down onto her bruised knees.

"Guy of Messaria," King Richard said, staring at her. "Ask her how many times she has been in this camp."

Guy did, and she jerked her head up at the sound of her own tongue. She spat. He asked her again. She looked down. The King of the English drew his sword with that distinctive scraping sound. Her head came up a bit; she answered with pride.

"Twice, lord King," Guy translated.

Richard struck a pose as if leaning on his sword. "And how many good Christian knights has she murdered?"

Guy asked; heard her recklessly proud "I sawed the ugly heads off two of the pigs," and said, "Two, lord King."

"Ask her what—ahh! I cannot. I have no stomach for looking at this creature! Yves! My armor! We shall return this murderess to her people! Sir Geldemar: well done, man! You have served us all well, and belike saved more lives— more heads! Valentin of Corinthia—speak you my tongue?"

"Caranthia," Leopold haughtily corrected, "and he does not."

Richard switched to German, and learned that Valentin understood it, though he spoke a Slovak tongue all his own. (And Leopold scowled.)

"I am sorry for your knight Sir Ludovic, Squire, and will pray for his soul. You are bereft of a good lord—but you are not alone, not alone."

Leopold scowled, while Valentin said *something* and, seeing that he was not understood by this kind lord of Normandy, said, *"Gratias, domine Dux."*

Richard smiled. "Well, that's fair Latin, at least," he said in his own tongue, and in Latin: "We hope that you can learn to speak the German which you understand, lad. French would not hurt!" For a moment he beamed at the young Slovenian, then, "I thank you all. Leave her just outside. Yves! My armor!"

Obviously dismissed, the others left, hustling the nameless murderess.

An hour later Richard's Pretty Girl hurled the ruined girl, alive and naked, back into Darum. She did not cry out.

"What a waste," Geldemar murmured, watching the body fly over the wall to impact with a great splatter inside the fortress.

"The whetted swords were given power over their heads and necks with the terrible blows of destiny and death; the unerring lances and severing arrows seized upon their bodies so that none of them escaped, save a few of those whom destiny had respited and to whose hearts fear had given wings."

—BAHA AD-DIN

NINE

Assault on Darum

That same afternoon one section of Darum's wall was badly weakened. The damage was worse, in fact, than the defenders knew.

Richard's own engineer had plotted and planned and sighted and even counted on his fingers. Meticulously Christian had caused Pretty Girl to be backed ten yards, then trundled forward two carefully-stepped paces. After taking more sightings and making further measurements, he assured his lord that the enormous boulder would hit the proper spot, and that the wall surely could not withstand the impact. They had after all put in nine hours of hard labor, on two successive nights, secretly bringing in the pair of boulders, each weighing two hundred sixty pounds. With great care the mangonel had discharged exactly that weight, four times.

The fourth missile, in late afternoon, was one of the two granite monsters. For once, it went exactly where Christian had calculated, and struck no more than a foot above the impact point he had plotted.

The crashing impact was enormous. Horrified and disbelieving, Saracen defenders were knocked from their stations while stones and mortar and dust fell. A portion of the wall buckled visibly, though it remained standing. Within the threatened fortress, orders were bawled and defenders rushed to that area to meet the attack that must follow the next shot of the accursed mangonel.

The attack did not come. Observers saw clearly that the

Franks were in dismay. Keen-eyed Turks watched closely and soon were all asmile. Excitedly they reported that the Franks' reactions were unmistakable: with that oversized missile the polytheist dogs had outsmarted themselves. The weight and strain had been too much for their hell-weapon—it was broken, useless! Allah is good—see the Frankish dogs wring their hands and shake their fists in frustration!

In the camp of the enemy, the tall helmetless man with the red-gold hair addressed the others gathered around the mangonel with him:

"Think you our marvelous jongleur act has convinced them how angry and chagrined we are—that Pretty Girl must surely be dead?"

"We can only hope so, lord king! *I* would be convinced, were I a Saracen observer!"

"Let us hope so, indeed. Very well. Now we walk sadly away from this poor engine, leaving behind only archers. Let the enemy think it has become no more than a bulwark for our bowmen. Tonight, however, we shall see that it is well guarded! And do pray that this part of the plan has worked, lads—and continues to work!"

That night he put the rest of his plan to the leaders of the crusading force.

His peers, insofar as the greatest knight in Christendom had any in all the world, listened to their captain-general's plan. They raised objections and arguments—the Frankish miners had not even finished their tunnel to undermine the wall; no man would wish to charge without his own banners...

Richard answered each argument with patience. After much persuasive talk on his part, they agreed. The knights would not be happy, but they knew the Lion-heart's military genius and they would obey their leaders. Such a plan had served Richard well in his own lands, during the awful civil wars there.

Next day, the fifth day of the siege, the bombardment of the westward wall commenced. Under a brassy-bright sky scattered with a few stringy little white clouds resembling painted smoke, Frankish archers and ranked catapults kept the defenders very, very busy all along that side of Darum.

True, that monster of a mangonel which Malek Rik called "Pretty Girl" was pulled up over on the eastward side, and had weakened two sections of wall there. But the Turks *knew* that the point of attack would be the west.

Over there, beyond the archers and cruel siege engines, just over the brow of a hill, they knew the infidel knights were massed. The Franks thought they were so clever, hiding beyond that hill, ready to charge while supposing themselves concealed! Yet from the towers of Darum's higher inner wall the defenders could easily make out the pennons and banners that clearly marked the lurking place of the fools!

The Muslims were several times wrong.

The crusaders were not fools or commanded by a fool, but by Richard of the heart of a lion, who had waged victorious assault on his first fortress at the age of eighteen. His knights were not planning to breach and charge the westward wall. In fact, the dreaded iron cavalry was not massed beyond that hill. Fifteen hundred men-at-arms were. They were even at rest—although they must hold aloft the banners of their noble betters!

Seventy iron knights were concealed a quarter of a mile from the wall on the eastern side, chafing in their mail, awaiting signal to charge. Another fifty were scattered here and there on that plain. Many had dismounted for the benefit of the watchers from Darum. The nobles were not happy to be bereft of the fierily bright banners and identifying pennons from off their long ashen lances. They rankled and chafed and grumbled, but they understood what was afoot and they did love chicanery and trickery!

Besides, the military genius of Richard had prevailed over their leaders, and they fell in line. The plan went forward.

Catapults were just able to loft the heads of the two Turkish archers over the westward wall. During the consternation those grisly missiles caused within the town, men grunted to load the second of the colossal boulders into Pretty Girl's throwing cup. Trumpeters stood ready to blast out the charge. Dismounted knights tried not to hold their breaths and strove to continue to act casual.

"Loaded and ready to launch, my lord."

"Do it, Christian."

"Launch 'er, boys!"

With a terrible creaking and the rushing upright of the huge pole to bang loudly against its stout stay, the 260-pound stone was slammed at Darum's eastern wall.

Wolfish men rushed to assist knights in mounting. Every crusader eye stared at the enormous boulder as it rushed into the sky, tumbled through the air—and smashed into the wall with a precision many of Christian's fellow engineers would not have believed possible. Indeed Christian was as elated as he was delighted.

So was his liege-lord, whose triumphant yell was drowned by the thunderous sound of impact. Stone and mortar flew and the thunder continued. So hard had the boulder lodged that it stuck fast in the wall for a long moment—and then fell ponderously back. With a new crashing thunder, it brought a broad section of wall down with it.

Richard the Lion-heart practically pounced into the saddle despite the weight of his mail and shield, and waved that bright shield on high as though it weighed nothing. The trumpeters blew for all they were worth. Horses lurched into movement while pieces of wall still tumbled and rolled, crashing, splintering anew, sending up a great cloud of dust between them and the sizable breach. Steel-clad men bawled out their cries and bent low over the necks of skirted, mailed chargers that began to trot and to lengthen stride into full gallop that made the very earth groan.

A new thunder rose on that plain before the walled town; the sound of thousands of iron-shod hooves pounding the earth at a dead run and the bellowed shouts of their fierce riders.

Armor gleaming, plumes and the skirts of their white surcoats streaming, the army of Christendom vanished into the billowing dust-cloud of earth and mortar. Horses stumbled over débris and some few fell. Others pounded on, leaping obstacles of broken stone beneath men yelling like the barbarians they were. Arrows flew about them and some found homes in armor and even flesh. Most of the Turkish archers, however, were rushing the width of the town from the west, where they had *known* the knights were; whence they had known the attack would come.

That mass of mailed men and horses burst from the dust into the town in a tidal wave of steel and yelling men.

On the fifth day of the siege, the twenty-second of May 1192, the might of Christendom entered Darum.

The town reeled in thunder and the lightning of flashing steel; amid screams and shouting, and the din of hooves and the ring of sword and ax and lance on armor and shield, flesh and bone. Mail jingled and chimed while horses cried out. Some put back their ears and bit savagely at Saracens even while their riders chopped and hewed a bloody path toward the central keep of Darum. Slashing, chopping swords and axes flung showers of blood on slain and slayers. Iron-shod hooves slipped in scarlet pools, skidded on hacked-off hands and arms, sent fallen heads flying up to fall again, stumbled briefly on fallen men, dead or no, and stepped squishily on them in their unstoppable progress.

Otto, Count of Guelders stared disbelievingly at the headless ax he had just somehow broken on the shield of a snarling man in silvered mail and spiked helm. Only for a moment he stared, and then he slashed the bearded Turk across the eyes with the jagged end of the helve before hurling it at another and drawing his sword in time to slash away a cut at his mailed leg. He resumed his grin and his hacking amid a rain of bright blood.

A few feet away, impressed that he had skewered no fewer than two Saracen men-at-arms on his lance, Geldemar of Wertheim hurriedly let go the long ashen stave and also drew sword. Neither he nor anyone else had any idea what it was he yelled as he chopped into the face of the man coming at his side and charged the worthier foe of a mounted Turk. Both their swords slammed into shields with frightful crashing sounds. Both men reeled, only a little.

Then the horses were plunging on, past each other—and the Turk ran full into the sword of Ludovic of Slovenia. It was wielded by the young Valentin who had been his squire. The Muslim never knew what killed him.

Elsewhere, snarling sons of Islam fell back from the flashing war-ax of the incredible Lion-heart, and were spattered with droplets of the blood that flew from that unusually heavy weapon. Richard did not bother to pursue them. He was single-mindedly bent only on hacking his way straight to the center of the town. His Fauvel continuing his lurching charge forward, ever forward.

Looming tall and silver-glinting in his mail and helm, scarlet plume fluttering, King Richard chopped anyone who chanced to be in the way. There could be no penetration past his madly swinging ax. The dreadful weapon smashed peaked helmets and struck heads so that they dangled hideously or flew on wakes of blood to roll in the street. It bit into the bodies of armored men as if they were rotten wood. Arrows whizzed down and failed to harm him. One struck his shield at an angle and caromed so that it took an attacking Turk in the cheek. He fell, groaning as he bled, wondering what had happened—until a great hoof came down on his chest. It crunched in and was ensocketed there for an instant before Fauvel dragged it out and carried Richard on. Neither horse nor rider noticed.

The Lion-heart was enveloped in the din of his own crashing weapon and the sound of Fauvel's snorting and the pounding of his hooves. He used both hands on the ax's handle, guiding the horse with body movements and pressure of thighs and knees or a touch of a heel. A small round shield or targe was strapped on his left arm just above the elbow; his great kite-shaped shield was slung from the saddle's trappings so as to guard his left side from knee to ribs.

Hawk-faced Turks blanched at sight of the outsized blade of his ax and the equally unusual length of its helve. No man should have been able to wield such weight in such a way. Yet this giant swung it as if it were made of mere rushes, his chain-covered arms twisting and the weapon looping and flailing, trailing blood.

Those capable of thinking got out of his way. Those on whom the unthinking battle-rage was strong or who knew that this giant had to be the infamous leader of all their enemies, shouted their rage and rushed to meet him—and found their own gory doom.

Yves of Anjou, Sir Reynald de Poitou, and Guy King-saver could only strive to keep up with their lord and sword-chop those he passed by as he slammed inexorably forward, a one-man force of scarlet destruction. Their lances were long since broken or wrested from their grasp in the bodies of transpierced foemen.

Behind them surged more shouting, hacking knights of Christendom on their stamping destriers. And behind them sounded the tramp of unmounted men. Those footmen who had not been part of the charade over the west side followed the knights. They paced grimly over the dead, slew the wounded, rushed into this building or that to clean up. Some fell to the arrows of ambushers waiting in those buildings, and were replaced by men who slew the slayers.

Not far from Richard, a well-mounted squadron of Templars fought. With them was Vulgrin of Montmirail, at their invitation. They slashed and hacked with no regard for the splashes of crimson on their formerly snowy surcoats. Blood was turning the dust of Darum's streets into rust-colored mud.

"Vulture meat!" one big north-born Knight of the Temple kept roaring, each time he slashed an enemy. The red battle rage was on him so that he had minimal awareness of what he was about or what he shouted. An arrow caromed off another's shield in such a way that it whickered across the berserker's face no more than an inch before his eyes. He did not notice.

Richard's shout carried even over the roaring din of battle and the screams and moans of wounded and dying men. At his bellowed order and then that of their own leader Anselm Mesnil, those superb warriors turned down a side street. They spurred their chargers with the momentum of man-gonel-hurled stones.

Arrows rushed down at them from the buildings on either side and the fighting monks seemed not to notice. Time later to pluck Saracen shafts from the armor of men and horses! Now they were busy with their mission from the lion-hearted king: they sought to find a swift way to Darum's innermost keep, that the siege might not be held up for days more in the taking of it. The young Frenchman, Vulgrin, rode proudly with them.

Richard swept on, a force unto himself.

His shining ax whirred over Fauvel's head to smash the hawk-lean face of a man attacking from the left, and rushed back to meet a sword-cut at his mailed leg. Ax struck sword-blade with a clashing ring and the symitar flew from fingers

164

gone all tingly and useless. Richard was five feet farther on and the swordless Saracen was just hefting his dagger when the shoulder of Squire Reynald's horse slammed into him. The Turk fell with broken bones.

Some following man-at-arms would dispatch him; he or another would snatch up that sword. Nor was he likely ever to know that the notch in his trophy's blade was put there by the ax of the Lion-heart.

Just after Richard passed a sort of alley formed by two yellowish buildings, no fewer than five mounted Saracen boiled out into the street.

They had no chance at the king's back, for Guy and Reynald and Yves were there, and upon them. The very first was a lucky man: Guy's sword struck his helmet at an angle, hard enough to knock the fellow unconscious. Thus he missed taking his death, for he fell back from the dashing hooves of the Crusader's mount.

Yves called Know-naught and another of the quintet each failed to deal a woundy blow, the sword of each banging off the shield of the other. While the Muslim rocked in his saddle, his horse charged on past, back the way the Frankish knights had come—and full into more of them.

They were delighted; Richard and his squires and former squire Sir Reynald were leaving precious few enemy for them to carve. The azure-surcoated Saracen received wounds from three men before he was sure what had befallen him. Reeling, he tried to strike, and overbalanced. He fell and was trampled.

Reynald meanwhile yanked his shield up in time to catch a silvery-flashing sword on its upper rim, then lowered it swiftly while he rose in the stirrups and chopped viciously. With a shriek of steel on steel his long blade raked down the side of the Turk's helmet and the camail or protecting curtain of mail pendent from it, to bite into the man's shoulder. He cried out in a high voice and his shield-arm swung down useless. At that he showed valor, striving to drive his sword at Richard's squire in an unusual cut: a thrust.

As if automatically, Reynald lowered his shield to catch the point even while he twisted and yanked his sword free of the fellow's maimed shoulder. Scales of steel armor flew as it came free; others remained imbedded in the wound. It gushed.

Arm twisting, Reynald slashed and this time drove links of camail into the neck it was supposed to protect. The very impact of the heavy blow sent the Turk flying from the handsome saddle he had had made for him in Cairo, and new mud was formed in Darum's street.

His mouth writhing so that he resembled a ferocious animal, clean-shaven Reynald looked about in quest of more foemen.

He was in time to see Yves slash an enemy leg while the sword of another slammed into Yves's helmet—and Guy's sword drive into the face of that Saracen. Yves rocked in his saddle, whose high cantle and pommel were designed to hold him there. The Saracen fell back, his face become a scarlet mass. His symitar flailed blindly. Guy's blade struck the hand that wielded it. Sword and hand flew away on a streak of scarlet.

"Yves!" Reynald called. "Are you all ri—"

He broke off; Richard's other squire answered the question by whipping his sword up under the chin of the meaty-faced man whose leg he had wounded. The blade chopped up into flesh and bone. The Muslim *spahi* or knight went all wide-eyed and fell backward with Yves's swordblade lodged in the bone of his broken chin. Yves must either release his grip on its hilt or be pulled from the saddle. The one was almost as unthinkable as the other and the reeling Yves had an instant in which to choose.

166

Reluctantly he let go his hilt and watched his sword go down with the enemy.

Nevertheless the five Muslim knights were out of the battle, dead or sore wounded.

"The king is in trouble!" Guy shouted, and spurred ahead in the direction of his pointing sword.

Seeing Yves on the point of swinging down to snatch up his sword, Reynald yelled. In his head-compassing helmet Yves glanced back to behold their fellow Christian knights pounding after them. In the face of that grinding wall of stamping horses. a man dared not dismount for his lost sword, even for an instant.

Yves was forced to haul his horse aside, to wait for an opportunity to regain his weapon or have it handed him by a footman. He drew dagger, just in case. It was a far cry from a sword, but over a foot of sharp steel could hardly be called merely a toothpick. At least he wore one of the newer helmets that afforded more protection. Almost square, it covered all his head and face, with slits for vision and a hole below for ventilation and voice, covered by a close-set grillwork.

Guy meanwhile was spurring into new conflict.

He had seen Richard beset by four spahis in quest of the most valuable head in their world; and worse, he had been struck in his upper right arm by no fewer than three arrows. Guy was sure that none broke through mail and the quilted jacket Richard wore beneath. Yet one stood from the inner portion of the king's right arm, near the elbow. It interfered with the movements of his weapon-hand. Nor surely would he dare risk giving up two valuable seconds to take mail-gauntleted left off the flailing ax to try yanking out the arrow in his right.

The Crusader spurred to the rescue, yelling and circling his sword on high to divert the attention of Richard's assailants—and Richard proved him wrong.

Swinging the ax across himself to the left with both hands, he let go with his left just as the ax-head struck a shield and carried it away—breaking the wrist of that Turk. Meanwhile the king's left hand leaped to clamp onto the slim shaft standing from his inner arm. His right, swinging back rightward, helped tear the arrowhead free of the quilted undercoat. Even as he missed the man he struck at and started a new looping swing, his left hand snapped around his weapon's long helve once again, and clamped. He had lost not a second, though at peril of seriously straining that mighty right arm. Still, men had seen him use his ax one-handedly before.

Nevertheless Guy of Messaria was working at shocking his lord's foes by his shouting and sword-waving. Now he added a third tactic, which he bellowed out in Arabic:

"Allah blister your bunghole, you camel's sons!"

Enraged, two men in high-domed helmets with heron plumes glared. Then both reined and kicked their horses in an attempt to meet him. The foremost, in a spring-green tunic over his beautifully linked mail, was turning in the direction opposite his shield. That exposed his right upper arm, and Guy's sword hewed into it. The second man struck in a great overhand chop and Guy showed his strength: he jerked his huge saddle-shield up to meet that blade—and thrust it at the gaunt-faced Turk.

The man cried out as his fist came down on the shield's top. His fingers sprang open and the curved sword rushed down at Guy's thigh. It struck painfully and slid away with a grating sound. The Crusader groaned aloud. He had felt the point even through his leggings of chain. He did not like the cumbersome things heavying his legs—and now vowed never again to enter combat without them!

As for wondering whether he might be bleeding . . . he had no time.

An outsized ax crashed into the back of his disarmed foe

before the fellow could bemoan the loss of his sword. The impact slammed him forward so that he fell into Guy's shield and leg. Then he was on the ground, writhing strangely and making stranger noises. His back was broken.

Richard's ax had been busy; between them they had downed all four of his assailants. He flashed his teeth at his squire from Messaria.

"Ho there, Cypriot! Have care with that shouting in Saracenic—my Fauvel might mistake you for one of them and bite your leg off!"

"I should teach him Arabic then," Guy retorted, also yelling amid the din though they were but a yard apart. "He'd be the fiercer did he recognize some of the insults these infidels shout! And would my good lord *please* pull the rest of those arrows out of his arm?"

"What arro-oh." Noticing the other two shafts, which had discommoded him not at all so that he had not known they were there, Richard let his ax hang loose at the end of that arm while he plucked them out. "Ha. I felt nothing. Bulky, this undercoat rather than jerkin, but worth its weight in . . . heads!"

"My lord—the other one got to you," a frowning Guy told him. "I see blood—"

"No. Theirs. See? It's only red!"

Laughing, the Lion-heart slung his ax and drew his saddle-sword. "Time I gave my arm a rest, though. Ah, how light this beauty feels!" He made the four-pound sword flash with a *wheep*ing sound through the air before he twitched Fauvel's rein. "We'd best either move aside or spur—here comes a pride of ferocious lions to run us down!"

Still laughing, he swung his mount and resumed his charge along a street strangely clear of foes for twenty or so yards. The king hurtled toward the nearest foemen. Guy had already glanced back to see mailed Christendom pounding along the street in their wake. With a gesture of his sword and a wild laugh in emulation of Richard, he sent his horse charging after the tall, tall king.

Two hours later the sun was dragging well down, looking as bloody as the streets of Darum, and Guy Kingsaver's sword-arm felt as if it were coming off. Covered in blood, he had no idea whether any of it was his own; he was too full of adrenaline to slow down and yet too numb to feel. He had taken blows and had felt arrows. The blood on his left thigh he *thought* was his own, but that leg was just as numb as everything else. He wore the blood of many men.

It seemed that days had passed since he had done aught save bestride a horse and ride and hack and block and duck and hack some more.

Once he had been unhorsed and about to be captured or slain, and it was a bellowing King of the English who came galloping back to disperse his attackers while the Cypriot dragged himself back into the saddle. Once his shield had been struck hard enough by a Saracen ax to splinter it and near wrench his arm out of its socket. Instead he stood in his stirrups and launched such a series of sweeping swordcuts that the burly and unusually strong Turk actually galloped off in quest of an easier foeman. The Crusader only just stopped himself from hurling his sword after the fellow. Another time the son of a Palestinian shopkeeper had flung a piece of rotting fruit at him, and such a lump rose up in Guy's throat that he had saluted the little demon and like to have gotten himself killed in that brief inattention to the business of war.

Brave little idiot, he thought, and met his attacker. When that was done and the Crusader's sword dripped fresh Paynim blood still again, he glanced over in time to see two galloping Turkish knights smash and splatter a similar brave little idiot without taking notice of his existence. He who

170

had challenged Guy was hurled aside by their chargers. There was no time for Guy Kingsaver to pause and touch the lad, even to learn whether he was sore injured or in pain.

Probably would have bitten the hand I put out to him, he mused. *Hates us all—and why not? It is his land, and we bring it only blood and pain and strife—Turks and we Christians as well.*

Thus he had thought on that occasion an hour ago, and then he must clap heels to horse and ride on, on to the next slashing conflict on the way to the conquest of this dungheap town. He knew that fellow crusaders were taking wounds and dying, but he saw only one knight slain. That was the aloof Dane, Rolfgar, who had no companions, never spoke to anyone, and seemed never to come out of his armor. Lonely fellow, Guy thought—and hadn't that lonely northerner come a long, long way to lie dead in a dirty street, in this hot clime so unlike Denmark!

At last, before the very inner keep of Darum, they were all caught up in a thicket of evilly keening, rushing arrows. They must needs fall back while Richard cursed and yelled for archers and cursed anew, and snarled, chafing, waiting for cross-wearing bowmen to come hurrying forward and commence laying down a barrage of goose-feathered shafts on the vantage-point of the enemy archers. Guy and others were glad for the brief rest. They dismounted with grunts and were wary of the arrows.

Richard's yeomen came, and they were the best: the archers of England.

All save one wore scarlet hose and low shoes, tied on the sides. Their shirts of mail were specially designed for their skill, with wide sleeves ending just above the elbows and the lower portion of the shirt forming a kilt that fell in steely scintillance almost to the knees. Each archer's mail-coif was topped by a round, iron-studded helm like a cap.

Each wore a large, oddly round collar of leather, and a leathern cuff or bracer on the left forearm from wrist to elbow.

They came trotting up amid a jingling of those full skirts of steel chain and a rattle of sheathed arrows. The quivers were slung not on their backs but aslant across their buttocks and upper thighs behind, so that feathers seemed to sprout just behind their right hips. None needed to be told why they were needed; here were knights and an impatient captain-general pinned down by Saracen shafts zipping down with sounds like angry mosquitoes. They keened down not from the wall of the keep up ahead, but from buildings on either side.

Indeed, the big iron-banded gate of Darum keep stood open. Just this side of it lay a Knight of the Temple. An arrow stood from his face.

The Templars had somehow got here before them all as Richard had hoped, Guy realized, and must already be inside the keep! Remembering the unpleasantness between Leopold and Richard after the fall of Acre, he hoped fervently that the Knights Templar were not so unwise as to raise their own banner above the final fortress of Darum!

As his men's big shields banged down and the yeomen braced their short props against the street, their leader glanced at Guy of Messaria as if to speak. However it was not the Human Crossbow but King Richard who gestured and barked his commands.

"Ah John, John! Just fill those accursed arrow-ports up there full of feathers, John you? We have business on the other side of that wide-open gate."

"More'n willingly, sire!" John of Lincolnshire in England said, and the short man gestured to the dozen or so archers with him. "Do it! Pepper the rot-arsed buggers, lads! Hit them archer-slits and keep on hittin' 'em! Guy—you lookin' to borrow a bow?"

"He's been using that arm as a butcher uses his cleaver all afternoon, John," his king said. "You leave him alone and get the job done. Guy Kingsaver rides in with me!"

From behind their tall standing shields those English masters of the bow began loosing their goose-quill shafts amid the constant *thung* noise of released strings and the hiss of departing arrows. Those sounds were followed by the high-voiced death-songs of the shafts. They rushed up seeking the slits from which a few enemy held down mailed knights.

The Crusader had taken note of the arrows loosed against him and his companions. He had seen none that were twice banded with red, nor had he expected to. Two blood-hued stripes formed the mark of one of the enemy's very best slayers, and Guy's personal enemy—Yarok, who was called al-Jazzar or The Butcher. He was surely with the main force of Saladin, whom they all assumed was far from here.

"Satan fart me out!" John of Lincolnshire cried, stamping one short leg. "Be that the best you can shoot? What are ye, secret agents for Silly-Sally-Din?"

His men either looked nervous or smiled or chuckled, depending mostly upon their apparent ages. They kept drawing arrows, nocking arrows, drawing string, and loosing arrows. Most bounced off the buildings flanking the gateway; some vanished within the slitted little arrow ports, and occasionally a stricken cry followed. It was answered by a triumphant shout from the westerners below. The Englishmen twanged their bows with new gusto.

"Saint George and England!" one of them yelled, and Richard smiled.

Amid the constant *thung-zzzt*, more and more knights and squires of Christendom rode up. Here came Yves, pushing through, saying "Make way, there!" and "Your pardon" by turns. Apparently unharmed, he had regained his sword.

Others grumbled but, recognizing Richard's squire, let him make his way to the fore.

After a couple of minutes, Richard looked about at them all.

"By the Cross, I want to be in that keep!" He raised his voice and bawled it out: "ATTENNND! Form into two columns. Those on the right shift your shields to that side until we are sure no more archers await us beyond that gate! Move now, hurry, let us be off!" And lowering his voice: "Yves! Beside me here on my right! Guy, you and Reynald, just behind. Let us boot these poor horses with such force that they'll be at the gallop by the third stride."

He was on the point of swinging into the saddle when the sound of mingled shouts and cheering arose from behind. They all looked back to see the cause. It fluttered high above helmeted heads: a scarlet banner with three golden leopards. It approached above that bloody street, while Richard stood watching, grinning. Not all men cheered, certainly, but all made way for the triple leopard banner of Richard Planta-genet.

A minute later Guy saw the big yellow-mustached Norman who bore it. He emerged smiling from the crowd, and with a bow of his helmeted head proffered the long lance. Also smiling, Richard wrapped his mailed hand around the shaft and hoisted it. More cheers arose.

"My thanks and God be praised, Wulf! All the way from this town's western side, are ye? Well, our trick worked. Here, Yves, do you hold this whilst I mount!"

Squire Yves did, and passed it to his lord once he was in the saddle. Richard planted the lance's butt in its saddle socket. The leopards waved high and men yelled their cheers. John o'Lancaster's men volleyed and volleyed, pinning those hidden Paynim archers they had not managed to wound or slay.

Then Richard the Lion-heart wheeled his big charger and

set off for the gate at a gallop, entering the keep of Darum as he should, banner fluttering triumphantly on high as befitted the captain-general of the crusade.

Immediately behind him was Guy Kingsaver of Messaria, and then more and more knights and squires. Only a few arrows struck their moving, two-sided wall of shields, for the English archers kept their Saracen counterparts pinned. Not one man took a wound. As they looked about at the few corpses strewn here and there within the keep, a man emerged from somewhere inside, pacing his horse. His surcoat was white, sewn with a large cross in red. He held up a hand, palm forward.

"Master Anselm!" King Richard shouted ebulliently.

"Lord King!" the Templar called back. "Your plan has succeeded. The keep is secured. Darum is ours."

While others cheered, Richard rode close. "It is your Knights Templar who have succeeded, Master Anselm. Accept my congratulations!"

Richard had learned not to thank the Knights of the Temple; they strove not for him, but for God, as on an earlier occasion he had been quietly told by their master and his Templar adviser, this same Anselm Mesnil. It was stated in the motto of those monkish knights: "Not unto us, O Lord, not unto us, but unto Thy name give the glory."

Abruptly the king wheeled his horse about and bellowed his words:

"What in the name of the Virgin is all that noise back there?"

The answer made him smile. The last of the Turkish armed force was falling back to make a final stand in their keep. From two directions, they had run full into the knights of Europe.

"Ho!" Richard bawled out. "Well then in the name of the Cross of God, let us make them *welcome!*"

175

It was then that weary men discovered new stamina and twitching arms became renewed to strength, and the business of red butchery began.

Within an hour the leopards of Anjou rose above the town's inner keep. Toward sunset on that May 22nd of 1192, the five-day siege ended, with the fall of Darum.

"Women suffered while on ordinary pilgrimage to the Holy Land, and they could hardly expect lighter treatment while on the crusades."

—RONALD C. FINUCANE, *Soldiers of the Faith*

"Loyalty can only be the consequence of loyalty. We are in one valley and those who think ill of us are in another."

—SALADIN

TEN

Pampered Captive; Unhappy Spy

The trouble with this godforsaken fortress was that there was nothing for her to do. Krak d'Entremont was far, far from an eastern palace or even fine home. It was hardly a castle, since it had been built by men for men—or almost-men, the monkish "men" who gave up money and possessions and their very manhood; their sexuality. The entire place was dim, day and night. Nothing adorned the bare walls. The utilitarian furnishings were not the least bit decorative. Even the food was little above standard.

It was a distinctly inappropriate place for Luisa de Vermandois to be.

Being the only woman here made it worse.

Of course there was that little ass Rosalba who had been Sister Paulina, but she hardly counted as woman. She was distinctly a girl, not a woman, and the girl was uneducated. She had chosen the convent, and the sterile, sexless life of a nun. Such a choice was beyond Luisa's understanding, and always had been.

Oh, she knew right enough now why Rosalba had so chosen; the silly girl just hadn't known better! She'd had no experience—then. The trouble was that she'd had no experience at anything, except being a farmer's daughter and an apprentice nun. She had all the learning and culture, Luisa thought bitterly, of a backwoods peasant. And, Luisa had swiftly learned, Rosalba had all the conversational skill of a milk cow. Or even a milk bucket.

The Lady Luisa was distinctly alone, despite Barak, who did have some culture and learning and was at least able to converse—and was sexually happy, surely sexually fascinated with her. That was pleasant. Luisa did love sex and sexuality and men and their hands on her and their cocks up her. On the other hand, Barak preferred to sleep alone. A bed in a barren monk's cell was lonely and chilly for a woman whose blood ran hot.

Another problem was that even though he was emir, Barak ibn-Yusuf had nothing for her here with which she could adorn herself or her "chamber."

A pigeon had borne them word from Lord Sultan Salah-ad-Din that a small cavalcade of carts and pack-animals was on its way with an armed escort. They were bringing niceties, proper eastern foodstuffs, condiments, some silks. Things to make life in this monks' fortress more livable, for people accustomed to and appreciative of niceties. Luisa was, and missed them.

So was Barak, but he was also a soldier.

How she had looked forward to the arrival of that shipment! With lovely new fabrics with which to decorate herself and her accursed monkish cell, she would set aside her noblewoman's ways and rights, and take up needle and thread. With decent food, perhaps she would even cook—only for Barak and herself, of course.

Excited as a girl, she pranced about like a maiden in anticipation of the May-day celebration—even going so far as to attempt to be kind to the little dolt who had been Sister Paulina. This elated new Luisa ruined a nice tunic from Richard's store to get herself up in skimpy, sexy bandeau and kirtle, in order to greet Barak privately as his woman. She had suckled him at her breasts, whose plentitude his dark hands kneaded and pressed; she had sucked him on her knees, lovingly fondling his furry balls and swallowing his seed.

Days passed . . . and they received another message.

Somewhere just over a day from here, Saladin's little caravan had run afoul of a band of marauders. Knights and their squires from Tyre, out to scout or to play, had spotted them. They attacked. The cavalcade was wiped out. The food and niceties were in the hands of the Christian queen and her new king, who certainly had no need of any of it.

For Luisa, it was like falling off a cliff. She was depressed for days.

She had softened the monk's *cell* all she could, with fabrics from the store Richard had left, and from this and that which Barak did possess. Too, the new dwellers in d'Entremont captured a few things in another raid on a little group of Frankish travelers, all male. This and that fell to Luisa, as magnanimous largesse of the new lord of d'Entremont. She opened out and slit the fine scarlet cloak while keeping out of her mind that it had belonged to a fellow Christian and European, now dead . . . because of her.

She re-seamed it into a sort of drape to cover a section of her chamber's ugly naked wall. It was only a mockery of decoration, and she moped and felt sorry for herself. What had she done to deserve such spartan surroundings and uninteresting food?

One of Barak's men had been slain during that raid, and in consequence no prisoners were taken. Once again the road below the fortress was cleared of corpses and indeed of any indication of strife.

Triumphant, he came to her that night. She saw the signs with expert eyes and understanding born of long experience. His chest was out and he was strutting. He more than wanted her, and she answered that desire, playing to it. With deliberate slowness she stripped for him, watching how more and more hot thick tube of hard meat bulged out from between his columnar thighs, thrusting boldly, adamantly—demandingly. Naked, she slipped to her knees before him.

She commenced to rub that bold erection softly, warmly between her palms. As the movements of her loving hands grew more and more vigorous, so did the throbbing of his cock. She moistened her palms from her mouth, rubbed and tugged and reached beneath to fondle the sac of his bollocks. The hair was coarse, for soft hair was a great rarity among any of these desert peoples.

His legs trembled and he sighed when she pressed her breasts around his flushed prick and moved her shoulders to caress it in that place of soft warmth. His kneeling lover kissed the head of his breast-warmed arousal, making a smacking noise with her soft lips because she knew he liked that. Cupping his balls then in both hands, she gave each delicate oval a warm kiss with gently-moving lips, and played her tongue over them. He twitched, swayed his hips, and emitted a happy sigh. On her knees, she began to move her head and to suck strongly.

That night she completed it with her mouth, sucking him off and swallowing it down, and both of them enjoyed it far more than a little, the kneeling woman and the triumphant commander who hunched his dark-furred loins into her lovely face with its cheeks sunken in suction. She nearly collapsed when he spurted strongly into her face, for her reaction triggered a powerful orgasm in her untouched cunt.

The Turkish complement of Krak d'Entremont resumed waiting, like hovering hawks, for the next group of pilgrims or knights small enough to be destroyed utterly. With pigeons ready to carry word to Saladin, men kept watch from the high walls.

A further trial for Luisa was the fact that Barak did not desire her every day or night, even for conversation. His visits to that accursed Rosalba saw to that, Satan rot the girl! He and his men were all fascinated by the short-haired blonde who had been a nun. She was kept inordinately busy.

The narrow path between the legs of the captured nun

had widened into a well-traveled roadway for Saracens.

As for her—well, now she *did* know better. Whatever the girl's ambivalent feelings and thoughts *(if she has thoughts,* Luisa sneeringly mused) and however much she might pray and feel guilt when she was alone—which wasn't often—she had responded to the clever and careful initiation Barak had designed for her. As if she were a filly, he saw to it that she was broken in for riding. Any filly accepted that, at least in time. Most seemed to like it. It was the life of a horse, to be ridden.

Rosalba proved a malleable filly. She accepted, and more. It began on that first night, with Barak's cleverness: the girl was not raped but was fucked, several times, and she was rewarded each time. Thus she was trained, conditioned. . . . Yet it went beyond that and soon they all knew it. As captive, she could suffer, or she could do that which she had discovered that she liked, and which brought rewards.

Soon she who had been Sister Paulina could not deny it: she was a horse that liked to be ridden.

Like? Luisa thought scornfully. *The little whore* loves *it! (So do I, of course, but that's different! God knows I never thought of wasting myself in a convent! I loved it the first time, when I was twelve, and was just sure I loved him, too, as well as his nice cock in me. This hell-damned war killed him. Since then—well, I did what a poor abandoned girl must, to get along in a cruel world not of her making. And now who is better in bed than I?)*

The trouble was that she was trapped in this revolting monks' castle, damn it, and under such circumstances she dared not have anything sexual to do with anyone save its master. And thanks to Rosalba, rot her loins, he was not infatuated with his "Lovisa" as he should be. Barak continued to sleep alone rather than with her, either after sex or without.

Luisa's was a lonely chamber and a lonely bed. Oh, he

visited that bed *almost* daily, or she his, but afterward they parted again and she must sleep alone.

God never meant for me to sleep alone! Not me!

Besides, almost daily was not the same as daily, or nightly either.

Luisa de Vermandois would have been quite happy to give Rosalba a little push off the high outer wall, or sprinkle glass in her food, or even slip a nice little dagger into her taut young self.

That, of course, Luisa also dared not do. These men were taken with Rosalba. Her pale, pale skin and sunny hair fascinated and delighted them. She was soft and obliging, lately a demure virgin and nun. She had become their pet. Only one person here could possibly wish her harm. Should anything befall her, Luisa would be the only logical suspect. Nor would Barak have any trouble explaining away her punishment to the sultan—*especially when I am dead and unable to speak on my own behalf!*

I their ally am become expendable—and their darling cute little whore is not!

Luisa de Vermandois was a woman, a spy who had helped their enemy—and a *Frank*. She was a Christian among Muslims. Who could ever fully trust or respect a traitor? She understood now that she was not indispensable, and the fact that she did not like it or feel dispensable helped not a whit. For word had come from the sultan: she was to remain here, since it was not safe for her to travel without goodly escort and he wanted no men to leave this important keep.

She was stuck here. She must make Barak happy, Satan blast it, and find some important service to render him and his lord.

As for Rosalba . . . *Just look at her,* Luisa thought, grinding her teeth, *only look at the simple-minded little cunt with attached body and empty head!*

Late on the day after her initiation, Rosalba had requested

that her crucifix be returned to her, for the wall of her cell. Her answer was a beating. That night she was neither used nor fed.

Next afternoon she was both used and well fed. The message was clear. Rosalba did not again mention a cross.

Allowed also to bathe, she dared complain when the new lord of Krak d'Entremont bade her keep her breasts bare. Accordingly she had received a severe breast-twisting, three scabbard-strokes across her rearward cheeks, and had gone without water that day. Now she was quite accustomed to the naked state of her tight but jiggly little titties, which made her quite fetching (damn her).

When she had made noises about a skirt, Barak had removed from his cloak a cord of braided cloth-of-gold. Now it fetchingly circled her hips, well below her navel. From it in front depended an ankle-length strip of white cloth. Its width was just about that of the length of her hand; a decoration, an adornment, and barely a loin-cover. Behind, a strip of cloth of equal width, black, trailed the floor or ground when she walked. It left bare the outer curve and more of each pistoning, youthfully taut buttock even while its color emphasized their whiteness, and how these men loved to watch that!

Black and white strips of cloth. So much for the former nun's former habit.

Barak had set a round-faced fellow named Ayyub to teach her their language. Ayyub worked overtime to teach her a few other things. Rosalba proved a good student.

That accursed meddling Mahmud, who had taught her to take his organ in her mouth and then to like it, had even turned over to her his handsome cloak of manganese blue. Barak did not allow her to cover her appealing self with it during the day, however; she was allowed to wear the mantle only at night, when the burning Enemy had left the sky and the air was grown chilly.

For some reason some semi-noble spahi had in his saddle-bag a pretty little ankle-bracelet, a thin golden circle. Now it jiggled and twinkled above Rosalba's ever-bare left foot. Ayyub had worn a ring set with Levantine turquoise on his littlest finger; now it adorned the middle finger of the captive who had become every man's girl. Barak's hoggish lieutenant, Yusuf, had worn a nice smooth chunk of handsome gold-orange amber on a little gold chain around his neck, for some reason—and now the thing appealingly glowed in the (ridiculously broad, Luisa thought) valley betwixt the girl's (pitifully little, Luisa thought) breasts. Apparently not wishing to be outdone, Barak's lieutenant Shawar had fashioned a bracelet for her from one of the gold bands that circled his curved sword-sheath.

Now the silly little crop-headed idiot's wrist flashed yellow with it, and she had no care that it had been utilitarian.

Some ass of an unusually handsome Turk, enamored of the common easygirl and at ease with the dullness of duty here, had created large earrings from silver wire taken in the latest raid on pilgrims along the road below. Naturally they were unusually showy, since her hair was so short. Thus they were glitteringly mobile with every faintest movement of her blond head. Her ears had been pierced before she entered the convent.

Thus was the nun-become-slut adorned, and Luisa had none of it. Except for the earrings. Earrings Luisa did have; extra large ones of gold, from Barak.

Each loop was two and a half inches in diameter; bold and very flashy. They were also thick and heavy. That fact Luisa had let Barak know during one of their intimate moments. He had stared, blinked his affront while his face showed his disappointment in her. Then he rose, dressed in stiff silence, and departed her company.

Luisa cursed—quietly—and she shed a few tears of self-pity. Then she gave the matter a bit of thought, and decided at once. She must; she was stuck here until Saladin said otherwise, and she was not about to try to "escape" and chance traveling alone. At least she had status here; at least he had not considered beating her as he had Rosalba, a mere captive.

And so she endured Barak's golden present with pride despite her discomfort, knowing that at least the big loops were unusually attractive. She wore them every day, taking them off only to sleep. And she was conscious that her life contained too many "at leasts."

They swung below her reddened lobes now, while she watched Rosalba's swivel-hipped, bare-footed pacing up the corridor. Luisa was concealed just within the doorway of her chamber. These inner precincts of this monkish haunt were dim, and with her room's door only ajar and no light on within, she could stand here without being seen as she watched others come and go.

The long white strip of cloth dangling before the girl rippled and creased and fluttered between her legs as she walked. Her emphatically white legs were visible all the way down with every step she took. Thus the "attire" Barak had chosen for her was mostly decorative; it covered only her lower belly and pubis. No easterner, she had not learned to walk unshod without coming down on her heels. Nearly naked buttocks trembled with every step. Her naked, pointed breasts were too taut to bounce, but jiggled merrily in a way Luisa knew was irresistible to men. She ground her teeth.

Her cold stare tracked Rosalba to her own room, and soon watched Barak's aide appear and enter the same room.

Mahmud is probably a good lover, too, Lady Luisa thought unhappily, and backed into her room to feel sorry for herself.

* * *

The little hair-of-sun did not speak much of his language, but Mahmud did not care. Not much was necessary. She understood some words, important ones, and signs and gestures, and she understood fucking. She also liked it, and Mahmud's stout cock. She was ready when he entered and soon he was in the saddle, contained within the broad sweep of her hips, riding low in the saddle and jerking back and forth so that her snowy thighs were straddled far apart. In moments clear, syrupy inner fluid was mingling with the sweat streaming along her thighs.

She sighed and jiggled beneath his rutting form. The brain-searing sensation of hard male tool slicing and slamming hotly into her was almost more than she could bear, every time, and always she wanted more.

Ah God, God help me—how I love it! And how good Mahmud is at it!—this pushing and pulling of my yarn, as they put it.

A feeling of happiness and fulfillment mingled with the lust that swelled and tingled in her frenzied body. Her eyes shone with it, were glazed with it. Her body spasmed and sweat beaded her face. Passion-delirious, the quaking girl panted. With her heels firmly planted she thrust powerfully up at him.

Sinful, all sinful, and she could not help it. She loved it. She could not get enough of it. She wanted them all, wanted every strong male organ in the fortress, wanted the strength and the desire of them—desire for her, for her.

Never had Rosalba or Sister Paulina felt so wanted, so needed. And God O God, how she needed to be needed! Toward sunset yesterday she had been allowed to go up on top and pace, to view the blood-red sunset surrounded by radiant orange and gold, and no one had put hands on her. She returned to her chamber, the former cell of a monk, and wept, for she knew fear that they did not want her any more, did not need her.

Then the lord Emir himself came to her, commander of them all and he who had made her woman, and she did her best to strangle herself on his big curving erection. She made him moan and look upon her with gratitude and surely love, and she was happy.

All tangled with that, somehow, was her almost constant feeling of guilt and knowledge that she deserved punishment. She sought punishment then, urging them to use and pound and ransack her body with theirs. She saw their delight and their appreciation and she fancied that she saw, too, their love.

Lying now under Mahmud, the kidnapped nun strove to impale herself to the ribs.

Her buttocks contracted into balls of muscle and her sleek hips pumped up and down, impelling her hungry lower mouth up and down his veiny cock. Clinging slick labia slithered along the thick long cylinder of that erection. She fucked her cunt on him to its limits. It quaked, that elastic-walled furrow, prick-dilated all the way to the rearmost nook of its recesses.

The searing heat of his glorious maleness burned inside her, far within her marshy tunnel. It vibrated in her, erotically, excitingly, so that she was all over tense and trembly. Her entire organism was seething with a devouring, demanding passion. Her hips were twisting in pleasure and need, completely out of control. They sought only to ravage the ever-hungry hole between her thighs and pierce the cervix buried so deeply within it.

He grasped her arms and drove harder, straining against silky inner muscles that fought to cling to his pistoning prick. The tension of her upthrusting arse and his own efforts kept it firmly, deeply entrenched in her so that their crotches were as if glued to one another. Hardly pausing in his strong surges into her, the lust-ruled man bent his head to nuzzle the yielding firmness of her breast, which was uprising even in repose. Aching for fulfillment, she tested her muscles by trying to surge breast and crotch both up to him.

He loves me wants me needs me needs me O pound me, fuck me hard and hurt me . . .

Passionately she hunched and clutched and urged and squirmed, until he groaned and tensed, grasping her arms so hard it hurt, and then he gushed his seed into her and went weak as they always went at this moment, and she loved that too. She felt strong at such times, and in charge, and at the same time very, very womanly.

She knew that she was important. She was worth something. She was worth fucking and spending into.

She lay there, her thighs pressed tightly together, squeezing the warmth Mahmud left behind once he had departed.

In a few minutes she was having doubts again, nervous, and the itch had begun so that she rubbed at her reddened crotch. But then Farouz came—wasn't this Farouz, with the sparse mustache and long thin fingers and long thin cock? Yes, she was sure that was his name. He smiled upon her and she turned over for him, and took him as always into the smaller channel that must have been created for long thin cocks, and she was happy while Farouz, squatting with bulging thigh muscles, buggered her until her mouth dangled loosely open in joyous response and a warm euphoric dimness enveloped her while he whipped slick sleek cock in and out of her wagging, back-thrusting ass and crammed her to bursting, and until he too emptied himself.

He departed, almost furtively leaving her a lovely little sweetmeat. She nibbled it gratefully and cleansed herself. She was just in time, for here was—well, never mind his name; he was smiling and he needed her. He came and he too wanted her from behind, but in the vaginal channel, and then he came again and soon left, and Rosalba was happy, sprawled with her legs pressed close together on the wet bulge of her reddened pubis.

* * *

Down the hall the lady Luisa of Vermandois also sprawled abed, also naked, and very alone. Staring with tear-misted eyes at the scarlet hanging that provided her chamber a pitiful decoration, she thought of Barak and of a big strong, once-innocent youth from the isle of Cyprus, now a superb lover . . . and she thought too of torturing Rosalba, as she clamped her engorged red nipple and twisted, twisted, while her other hand raked and clawed at her genitals.

"The rôle of most non-combatant women was passive, but there are clear indications that women sometimes took a more active part in the fighting. . . . During the Third Crusade . . . three Frankish women 'fought from horseback and were recognized as women only when captured and stripped of their armor.'"

—RONALD C. FINUCANE, *Soldiers of the Faith,*
1983

". . . there were indeed women [among the Franks] who rode into battle with mailcoats and helmets, dressed in men's clothes."

—IMAD AD-DIN, 1192

ELEVEN

Some Unwelcome Surprises

The battle for Darum was over, save for a little cleaning up here and there, of concealed enemies. Some had become snipers with bow and arrows, or vipers lying hidden and waiting to strike at any who chanced close. Richard sent loud-cryers about through the town, urging them to come forth in surrender and promising that they would be neither slain nor tortured.

Guy Kingsaver had no need to take part in that activity, and he was weary. After hours and hours of combat, his clothing was drenched and sodden. Sweat plastered his hair to his head. Yet it was as if he had no choice; as if he could not help himself. Despite his weariness, he felt compelled to remount and ride back through the fallen town.

Stupid, he mentally chastised himself—but he had to know about the boy who had dared throw a piece of rotting fruit at him, a mailed Frank mounted high on his snorting charger and dripping blood. A goodly brave lad, a Palestine native to whom the ruling Turks of Saladin were just as much foreigners and nearly as alien as Guy and the other Europeans. The Crusader was not riding back to chastise the boy. He could not have said why he hoped the brave lad was all right and needed to know; it was that he had to.

Thus it was that he was privy to an astonishing revelation. He came upon the man-at-arms, one of Leopold's Austrians in an overlong orange tunic, staring down at a sprawled figure. He had made the scandalous discovery about the one knight Guy had seen go down in death: Sir Rolfgar of Dane-Mark. Gazing down at what he had uncovered, the fellow hardly noticed when Guy swung down from Deukkak's back to join him in staring.

Rolfgar may or may not have been a Dane, though the usual knight's close-cropped hair was not red as one expected to find among those of that cold land. Certainly Rolfgar had not been a knight. Just as certainly, whatever the dead warrior's name had really been, "Rolfgar" had been even more brave and more lonely than anyone had thought—or more stupid. For Sir Rolfgar was no sir, nor indeed a man.

Guy stood staring down at the lean face, the staring dead eyes, the open mouth on which blood had crusted. They were a woman's eyes. It was a woman's soft mouth. These were a woman's smooth, smooth cheeks, pale because "Rolfgar" had retained the head-encompassing helmet at all times. Must have taken a vow, like some monk, some men had opined. Aye, Guy thought now. A vow not to reveal her identity—her sex!

Rolfgar had been a woman. French, probably—that is, a descendant of the old Frankish people, judging by that nose.

The man-at-arms said something that had the sound of a question. Guy did not understand, and said so in French. The man looked at him, and his eyes widened in a middle-aged face without scars save the usual ones from smallpox.

"The Human Crossbow!" he said, in French.

"Uh, so I'm sometimes called. What did you say before?"

"Oh." The fellow had a hard time stripping the gaze of his wide eyes off the well-known hero from someplace called Cyprus. At last he looked down at "Sir Rolfgar" once more. "I said, 'Think you this be a youth?'"

Guy shook his head. *"Non."*

"Is . . . is it possible that this are a woman?"

"Oui."

194

"God's blood," the Austrian said, "what a waste!"

Guy gritted his teeth. Aye, was a waste, all right. But he hated the words and this man for saying them. What a callous remark!

"Why in Jesus's name would a woman want to put on armor and a helmet and come here and *fight?*"

This lean, lean man, Guy was reasonably sure, had known no such desire. He was here because his lord had called in the vassals to accompany him on crusade, for such was the power of any lord. He promised protection; the lesser nobles and vassals and serfs promised and owed service. It did not matter. Guy of Messaria had no answer.

Who could know why this youngish woman had done what she had done, donning armor and taking up the name and business of a man, this woman who had taken the cross and fought and died as a man—a knight?

"Only she and God knew," Guy said. "Now only God knows. Come, give me a hand—we cannot leave her here." He added "Git!" to a snuffing, yellowish dog and the two men bent to lift the dead "knight."

"Uh. Nearly's heavy's a man—pleasure to meet you, uh, Human Crossbow—uh . . . I forget your real name, milord."

"Into this building, for now," Guy said, and they bore the dead woman into a wrecked wineshop as he directed. "Guy. Guy of Messaria—Cyprus."

"Oh yes," the gaunt-faced man said. "Right. Guy—call you Guy Kingsaver, don't they, milord?"

"Aye, but no need to call me 'lord.' My father was Peter, a farmer. Yours?"

"Dead. Name was Luitpold, same as the Archduke's. Forester. I worked a little land. My name is Otto, Guy Kingsaver."

"I hold me good friend of Sir Geldemar of Wertheim, Otto Luitpold's son, and call you friend too. Let us leave her here for now; I have business. Poor woman, to come

195

into all this and then to die! Tell your baron of her when you see him, Otto. Why not just avoid telling others—I like me not the thought of many men coming here to stare at her in curiosity, passing remarks, perhaps to—well, to touch her."

"I understand. Got me a wife—and a brace of pretty decent children, too. I take your point. Oh—you still a single man, ain't you?"

"Aye. But about her, Otto. *Rolfgar* lived and fought as a knight, and deserves respect and Christian treatment and burial."

"Our secret, then?" Otto straightened up from the mailed corpse, looking delighted at sharing a secret with this renowned young hero so many talked about. Guy nodded and Otto did, then said, "A man'd love to see you pull that bow of yours, Guy Kingsaver."

"I doubt me whether I even could," Guy said, pacing out to his waiting horse. "My arm is so tired from sword-work that it's still trembling and feels weak as a kitten's leg." He lifted foot to stirrup. "Besides, the bow I left outside. I am squire to the King of the English, and acted as swordsman today, not archer."

"Ye acted as a *knight* today," Otto said. "It's a knight ye'll be too, with me and everybody calling you 'Sir Guy.' And I for one will be real pleased. Otto Luitpold's son salutes you, Guy Kingsaver!"

Guy gazed down at him, with a whimsical little smile tugging at the edge of his mouth. He had still not gotten used to this business of being a hero and well known. Whether he liked it or not, he always seemed to suffer an attack of modesty and embarrassment when someone was as obviously adulatory as this Austrian peasant—this fellow peasant. Nor did he ever know what to say.

He lifted a hand with a soft clink of his mail. "I salute you, Otto, warrior and crusader!"

While Otto's jaw dropped, Guy rode on. He was thinking not about Otto, of whom he'd had ill thoughts at first, but about a nameless woman who had called herself Rolfgar. *And are there other such among us?*

He thought about that, wondering, as he rode along a street in which Deukkak's hooves made squishy sounds in blood-red mud. The horse he had named "Crusher," in Arabic, needed no guidance: he stepped around or across swords, broken shields, axes and spears, and corpses. Men were removing the bodies from the street, and Deukkak paced around them, too. The destrier was happy to bear his master slowly, after the strain and din of battle. He and his rider heard the sounds of wailing, for some of the Turks had women with them and long-time natives of Darum, too, had been slain by warriors of both sides. Once Guy paused to point an accusing finger and tell a pair of men-at-arms in Richard's colors to leave the corpse alone.

"Let the poor wailing woman have her man, to mourn and bury her own in her own way."

He pretended not to know that the two Poitevians were intent on searching the corpse for loot. They might have had plans concerning his truly skinny wife, too, poor woman.

They gave him surly looks, but said nothing. Both of them knew who he was, and it was not as the heroic Human Crossbow that he commanded their respect and obedience. He was squire to their liege-lord Richard, and his friend as well.

The woman tugged her husband into the little house with its arrow-studded outer wall, and slammed the door.

"That poor widow is a citizen," Guy said. "Now she's under our protection. Oh, I'll tell ye this—I passed an alley not ten yards back, with a couple of Saracen knights lying dead in it. Why not fare ye there and check those bodies— they might have been carrying despatches from Saladin, or something."

197

Both men grinned and departed at speed. Having distracted them from this widow and her house by inviting them to go loot a couple of warlike corpses, Guy rode on. A bony gray cat, sniffing at a severed hand lying against a building, fled at his approach and passage. Within twenty yards he recognized the shop he sought. There was no sign of either of the lads, the one he had seen trampled or the one he now sought, who had been merely bowled aside—Guy hoped. The street had been cleared before it, mostly, and the Crusader nudged Deukkak over to the door. Braced on the inside too, he had little doubt. The sign bore a reasonably well drawn picture of a couple of figs and a pomegranate, fresh sliced and dripping violet. A fruit-seller's shop, then.

Guy swung down and rapped on the door, which was of good wood. It was also not braced on the inside at all, and swung partway in at his knock. He waited. No one called an answer, and no one came. He knocked again, and after a moment he used one foot to ease, not kick, the door the rest of the way open. He tried a halloo in Arabic. That brought no reply; not a sound.

Strange. Fled, I hope, not dead. And he stepped into the doorway. He did not see the boy he sought.

In the first two seconds he had a glimpse of a dim room about ten by ten feet in size, with a couple of worn carpets on the floor and several trestle tables and bins for the display of fruits. The arched doorway was thus ten feet away, in the right rear corner. In it stood a man, not uniformed but wearing a turban and a striped jallaba. Only just visible behind him was a girl or woman, peering at the visitor with large dark eyes. She was looking at Guy over the man's shoulder; the man was looking at him along the arrow nocked in his drawn bow.

"Wait!" she cried, high-voiced. "He called out in Arabic—"

198

The man paid her no heed; in the third second he released the string. Before the fourth second had passed the arrowhead slammed into Guy Kingsaver's chest with a real impact that made him gasp and stagger backward out of the doorway with the arrow's dove-feathered shaft standing from his chest.

"Please grant me your pardons, milords," Templar Master Anselm said, "but I need brief privy converse with the captain-general."

The archduke of Austria half-turned to glower at the fiftyish man with the long, long lines in his face; Richard looked at the warrior monk across the broad shoulder of Leopold. The latter, in the bricked courtyard of the town's keep, had been stating his strong case for the division of Darum between them. As yet no banners flew from the high walls.

"Privy converse, you say."

"Aye, my lord. With apology to my lord Archduke," Anselm said, making a goodly bow of his head to Leopold. "Will be brief."

Before Leopold could speak harsh words, Richard replied quickly. "Who could say ye nay, Master of the Temple?— was you and yours who took and held this keep for us ere ever we were able to hew our way to it! Your pardon, my lord," he added to Leopold, and strode past the short thick man. One long arm of the King of the English guided the other man around and into a decorated archway.

Leopold stood staring after them, naturally suspicious but scowling no longer. Richard's words were true, and the archduke was none so small as to resent an interruption by the Master of the Knights of the Temple.

On the other hand, he thought, *this private chatter had better not be about the disposition of this town!*

It was. "My lord," Anselm said very quietly, turning to

look directly into Richard's eyes once they were out of the archduke's hearing, "once you've heard my words you may not be so happy with me and mine."

"If it were possible for that to be so, Anselm, neither you nor the Temple would need worry about Richard's ranklement!"

The Templar did not smile. "Richard, you mentioned that brave lad Vulgrin to me, and we invited him to ride with us. He was right glad, and truly valiant. Also impatient, in his youth. I make it that he gave no thought to the possible momentous meaning of his act, but it was he who rode first through yon gateway into this keep. We were close behind. Nevertheless, was he who entered first."

Richard stood staring into that long-lined, leathery face so like that of an aging hound. The Lion-heart's smile had gone but his face was seemingly relaxed in contemplation. "Umm. Technically under my orders o'course, as you accepted them and he was—technically—under yours. Nevertheless ... hmm." A slight nod, a couple of fingers to the lip. "A knight of *France* first entered Darum's keep and so—technically!—it fell to him."

Anselm's nod was slight and his sigh great, but he was strong enough to continue to look directly into the eyes of the high lord he called by name. He barely whispered the word: "Aye."

"Damn and blast," Richard said, "without pardon!"

Anselm almost smiled. "Surely God understands, Duke and King."

"So. Doubtless the lad has not even thought on it, as you say. Yet he could lay claim to this town, for France. And Burgundy's dear darling duke."

Again Anselm Mesnil nodded, this time in silence. The Master of the Knights of the Temple would say nothing against Duke Hugh or even much of anyone else, even to Richard his friend.

Suddenly a little smile toyed with Richard's face. "On the other hand, there is a happy aspect—Leopold is going to be sore disappointed if not worse!"

Anselm gave him a look and shook his head. "Tsk tsk," he said, in the manner of a disapproving father.

"Oh yes I know," Richard said, "unworthy, unworthy! Speaking seriously, however—there is a way. It encompasses all, as I see it. Attend me and see if you find fault. This is a small town and of little consequence, but it is here in Outrémer . . . in the Kingdom of Jerusalem. Never mind that neither Hugh nor Henry was here for the siege and the battle—but may God remember and hold them remiss! Neither Leopold nor Vulgrin nor Burgundy would object—or dare object aloud, at any rate—were I to *give* Darum to the new King of Jerusalem!"

Very slowly the Templar's straight mouth commenced to widen and its corners to lift. His eyes came alight.

"Ah Richard, my good Christian lord! What a noble gesture!"

Grinning, Richard said, "Isn't it! *Un beau geste!* How noble of me!" He looked about. "Oh well. This rat's arse of a middenheap town is hardly important to me, or to Austria either. Peradventure 'twill do Cousin Henry some good. I shall send someone straightaway with a message to the King of Jerusalem—on the morrow. Guy, perhaps, when he's had a chance to rest. And how grateful Henry is going to be! Particularly if we make no mention of the Vulgrin matter."

"More brilliant strategy, Richard! As to that last . . . what Vulgrin matter?"

Richard squeezed the warrior monk's shoulder with a big hand whose grip Anselm felt even through his mail. He swung to return to Leopold, paused and glanced back.

"Thank you, Anselm."

"I did not expect to hear that from my lord captain-general!"

"Did you not! Yet you sought to prevent my making a fool of myself and giving rise to even more trouble for this plagued crusade. I shall remember."

And King Richard wheeled with a flutter of his long and badly besmirched surcoat, went back into the courtyard to give the archduke of Austria some news he was not going to embrace with love.

"In fact, after five days of fierce fighting, Darum fell on 22 May 1192, one day before Henry and the Duke of Burgundy arrived. But, in a fine gesture, Richard at once handed the captured town to the new lord of Jerusalem. Now that there was a new spirit of co-operation among the Christians they would surely succeed. This time, moreover, they would not be hampered by the winter mud and rain."

—JOHN GILLINGHAM, *Richard the Lionheart*, Times Books, 1978

TWELVE

Kimri

Guy Kingsaver did not quite fall. Adrenaline pumped through him and he felt at once the sensation of light-headedness and pervasive, prickly heat. He had been shot. He had seen the arrow and heard the twang of the bow's gut-string. Far worse, he had felt the blow of the arrowhead striking him. It was shock and the heavy impact that staggered him.

He looked down at it. It stood straight out from the center of his chest, quivering with his breathing.

Breathing.

He was alive. God did not care, but armor did.

He lifted a hand to close it on the arrow's shaft. He pulled. The steel head came free, and it was the color of steel. There was no blood. His coat of linked chain over a quilted jerkin had served its purpose. He was alive. Further, he was unwounded. Far more importantly, he was not even scathed.

He was probably bruised; nothing more.

For a moment he felt a little weak in the knees, as the adrenaline rush left him. Then he drew his sword. The long drawing motion was accompanied by a scraping sound, steel blade along wooden sheath covered with boiled leather.

Shot but unwounded, he grew even more daring. With his sword in his fist Guy of Messaria stepped back into the shop's arched doorway, ready for just about anything except what he encountered.

Across the room, in the other archway, the man who had tried to kill him stood loosely, bow dangling, as if relaxed.

His mouth was working though he said nothing. For the first time Guy noticed that he wore an empty dagger sheath. With wide eyes he stared at the Christian he had shot. So did the young woman behind him.

Then he dropped to his knees, and shuddered, and fell face forward to lie still but for the twitching of his lower legs. A dark patch discolored the back of his tunic. It was growing like a fast-blooming rose.

Now the Crusader stared at the plump young woman who gazed back.

The first thing he noticed was the dripping dagger in her tawny fist. The color of the falling droplets matched that on the back of the prostrate man's tunic.

It was strange that this was the first thing he noticed about her, since except for exceedingly low-slung *sirwal* or balloon-pants in faded, diaphanous yellow that shimmered over her legs all the way to the insteps, she was entirely naked. Unless one counted the bronze bracelet or large silver earrings or the burnt-orange dye surrounding her nipples in a dark, provocative circle, and Guy Kingsaver did not. Such adornments did not constitute clothing or help cover nudity; they enhanced it.

Looking at him, she tossed the dagger away in a deliberate gesture to make sure he understood that she was disarming herself.

"You cried a warning," he said in her tongue, "and you slew him. Why?"

She held her arms out from her body, palms open and up, in a gesture that showed she was unarmed; a posture of submission.

"I recognized thee, for I have seen thee only in thy armor. This was not a good man. Thou art a good man—though when first we met thou didst lie to me."

Guy could only gaze in puzzlement at this dusky girl in her late teens. "When . . . first we . . . met."

She put her head on one side coquettishly or question-ingly, he was not sure which, and her great mass of black, black hair shifted, flowing over her shoulder and along her arm. "Aye. Thou saved me . . . my farm . . . my sheep."

"Sheep," Guy said stupidly. He had no notion as to where he had seen . . . met! . . . this plump daughter of the Lev-antine desert, or who she was. How could he admit it, though, and ask? "But I—lied to you?"

"As thou departed, I asked thee thy name." A tiny smile touched her lips and her face took on a mildly defiant look. "A girl likes to know the name of her first lover. Thou called back that thou wert Malek Ric, of the lion's heart. I believed thee then. Now I know otherwise. For he is not from Cyprus, and has strange hair the color of the gold and of sunset, and eyes of an impossible hue—the sky."

True, and Guy knew who she was. That is, he remem-bered the occasion, though not her name. That was not surprising, since he had never learnt it.

He had been separated from the rest of the army when he had come upon the scene: her little farmhouse in the middle of nowhere, the dead animals, the two grinning Turkish soldiers. After he had saved her from rape and dispatched the pair of Saladin's soldiery who had slain two of her sheep, she had given herself to him—no, she had urged herself upon him.

"The sultan's men," she had told him less than a year ago, in early November, "came and took my brother into their army. Only a month ago, my father died. Today those two found me. They slaughtered two of my sheep and said that I would come with them as their woman. I ran." And she had said, "Your coming here was the will of Allah. Perhaps it is His will that you abandon your warlike com-panions and take up peaceful ways on a farm?"

He had told her that such could not be, but that since she was alone she might come with him. He guaranteed that

207

she would not be a slave among hs people. She had shown rage when he had referred to "your sultan," insisting that Saladin was "not *My* Sultan! He is a Turk, and from Egypt!" Then he had prepared to take his leave, assuring her that he would neither rape nor slay ... and of a sudden he saw hurt in her large brown eyes, and then tears.

"I was frightened," she had whimpered, "but at least I knew that I was going to know what it was like, at last. And you, Frank-from-Cyprus-who-speaks-the-tongue-of Allah, do not even *want* me!"

Then they had loved—or rather fucked, there on the ground near her home. He had dared not remove his armor, though it abraded and doubtless bruised her. Both of them had loved it just the same. As he was leaving to return to the rest of the army, she had called out to ask his name. On the instant, on a whim, he had decided to give her a gift, something to warm her thoughts in the future. He had told her that he was Richard.

Then he had gone his way, and thought of her no more.*

And the future had come, not quite seven months later. Here she was, not on her farm but unaccountably in a little shop in Darum, and she had slain him who had sought to do death on Guy—slain with his own dagger a man so stupid as to think her only the girl he kept nearly naked, and had thought himself safe with her behind him.

"And I never took off my armor," he said with a tiny smile, murmuring the words.

She smiled. "I was bruised—and gloated over those bruises! A good man happed along that day, and saved me from *them,* the Turkish overlords." She turned her head to spit ritually. "Then he took me, for l needed and longed to be taken. But not by them—I gave myself to a hero and savior." She looked down. "No child came of it, however.

*In *The Passionate Princess* (The Crusader #2), chapter 15.

I hoped it would, even though that would have been... troublesome."

"I'd think so," he said, most uncomfortable and yet just where he wanted to be. "A girl alone, with a farm to tend. Aye, I told thee I was King Richard. As a gift, that you might think thy first man was someone of great importance."

Her large brown eyes went larger. "Oh, but he *was!* He still is! My first... and now... now..."

She did not look away as he might have expected, but only glanced down at her feet before meeting his eyes directly, with her cleft chin up. Putting her head a bit onto one side, she asked, "What truly is his name?"

"My name is Guy, called Kingsaver, son of Peter. I really am from Cyprus, a place called Messaria—what is the matter?"

"Matter!" she echoed, wide-eyed. "But I know of thee! Thou art a hero of the Franks—as well as of me! These Turks well know your name, Guy Kingsaver, and your bow, and so do these dogs of collaborators." She spurned the dead man with her bare foot, and Guy noted that her toenails had been painted with henna. "Ah, how they respect but hate thee!"

The usual embarrassment washed over Guy, and he swallowed, trying to fight it back. "Oh," he said, remembering. "This meeting is happenstance, for—"

"The will of Allah," she said, and added "'Ihhamdulil-lah!'"—Praise be to God.

"When I passed this shop earlier, I saw two lads. One I saw die, run over by Turks on their horses. The other was knocked aside. He is a brave boy who I hope is not harmed. Know you aught of him?"

She shook her head. "Nay. This town holds many boys, and girls as well. None lived here; only *he*—" and again she touched the dead man roughly with her foot, "and I, whom he sought to make his *hhareem*-girl, his odalisque,

209

as if he *were* someone, this swine. His assistant lives elsewhere, but came not in to-day."

Helplessly, hopefully he said, "Neighbors...?" but he trailed off.

She looked down. "I am sorry. I know none. In how many houses would thou query after him?"

I am never likely to know, then, he thought, and heaved a sigh. Suddenly his arm leaped out to point at her. "You will fetch a—what is your name?"

"Kimri."

A whimsical smile touched his lips. "Kimri. That is 'dove' in my language," he told her. "Oh aye, I remember our first meeting, Dove with the heart of a lion, who slew him who tried to kill me out of hand! And I never removed my armor that day with you—I dared not. Well, now I dare, for Darum is ours and you and I are both safe, Kimri, safe. We will away from this place, you and I! First, do you cover yourself—a cloak will do, for once we are in another, better place, I will only bid thee put it off or pull it from thy body."

For the first time, Kimri truly smiled. "O my love, my first and true love and savior! From thee would I welcome such rough stripping! A moment only!"

Only a little longer than a moment later she was draped, enveloped in a man's long cloak of stripes, red and black and green picked out in white, and they hurried out of the shop. He paused with a foot in the stirrup and turned a little smile on her.

"Dare I trust thee behind me, Dove with the heart of the lioness?"

She laughed and her eyes danced. "My savior but jests, for that one inside deserved what I gave him. But bind my arms if you will, or hold me before thee..."

Chuckling, he swung up and reached down a hand for her.

Then she was astride his horse behind him, in her excitement wickedly thrusting her loins against the high back of his saddle while her arms encircled his steel-encased form. Back through death-filled Darum the Crusader's destrier bore them, and men watched when the cloak furled back to bare a dusky, muscular leg above painted toenails. Into the keep Deukkak paced, with Guy sitting tall.

The third man they saw was taller than tall, with blue eyes and hair the color of old gold or of sunset. He threw up a long arm in greeting.

"Ah, Guy! I'll want to see you on the morrow, once you've rested! I have a mission—hmm. Looks as if ye'll not be resting. Dangerous looking captive ye bring in, eh?"

"A native, my lord, not a Turk. Natheless, methinks I should question her..."

"Oh certainly, of course, of a surety. Question her. Oh, aye," Richard the king said, with great merriment in those cerulean eyes. "Question her, aye. Probably take most of the night too, I'd wager. Poor Guy! A dedicated man and squire, though. Well, Squire... find you a chamber in this place, and do you set your shield before the door. 'Tis a king's warranty that ye'll be disturbed in your *questioning* only by some tame local serf bearing a bit—just a bit, mind—of food and mayhap, only mayhap, a bit of ale or even wine. Get on now, whilst chambers remain.

"Ahh... y'aren't in pain, are ye Guy? I see me how that mean-looking spy to be *questioned* has a death-lock on ye, around your poor midsection..."

"My thanks, lord King. I will survive, lord King."

"Oh, that is good to know."

Richard waved a hand of dismissal that also urged Guy to be on about his business. As the Messarian rode off with the girl clinging to him, Richard turned back to the Earl of Leicester and murmured, "How *does* that homely Cypriot lad do it, Robert? He finds them positively everywhere.

Clinging to him with love in her eyes, I vow! And what must a mere king do? Plan, plot, and look only at ugly furry male faces . . . Arrh! To have been born a peasant of Cyprus!"

Robert of Leicester rolled his eyes and did not deign to comment on such nonsense. He was an old friend, and knew: If anyone reveled in the several rôles, all important, that were his, it was Richard Plantagenet.

The phrase "Oriental splendor" was a cliché that unfailingly called up a mental picture. Guy and Kimri had discovered a chamber of Oriental splendor within Darum's keep. The Crusader's shield, leaning against the wall just beside the door outside, made it his, for this night at least.

Within that large and airy chamber he and Kimri were agog at sumptuous patterned carpets woven by loving hands, ornately patterned wall-hangings with dangling tassels, pastel columns supporting gentle arches, furniture of intricately carven and filigreed wood, and brass, and black iron.

"A Sultana's palace!" she cried, racing from caressing an intricately carved table of pecan wood inlaid with mother-of-pearl to running her hands over a low divan off which rich silks drooled in folds that trailed their tassels on the floor inlaid in cinnabar and cream. "Oh! Ohh!" And she twirled in unselfconscious girlish joy that afforded her companion an inspiring view as the cloak stood out from her. He did not forbear to look at the pirouetting plumpness thus revealed.

They have not, thank God, starved her!

"Nay," he said, "only—"

"Look! Water—a sunken bath—*bath* water! And *unused!* Oh!"

In a flash she had dropped the multistriped cloak and was hopping along in her efforts to drag off her ballooning pants both legs at once. Before he had a good view of richly jet-

212

furred loins and strong unshaking buttocks above sturdy thighs, she was a-splash in the water. Kimri laughed and splashed about like a child.

No longer weary but still sweat-encrusted, a grinning Guy Kingsaver joined her as soon as he could rid himself of a surplus of warlike clothing.

After that they were two children cavorting . . . but not for long, for adult attributes and pleasures were revealed to them both. After that matters rapidly became involved, and bathing became secondary to laving each other with oiled water, mingled with much fondling and nuzzling and worse. Hands slithered intimately hither and thither, exploring and caressing, eliciting sighs and giggles, moans and gasps.

"Oh!" she said, staring big-eyed down into the water, "sea serpent!" And she grasped it so that he gasped. A moment later she said with mischievous merriment, "Oh my, this must be very dirty. Best clean it well, with both hands!" And she went after the "sea serpent" with both tawny hands. It grew.

"Look!" he cried, just as silly-merrily. "They float!" And he slid lower into the water to go nipple-nibbling until she was first squealing, and then moaning and sighing. Below the water, his hands explored other, non-floating aspects of her anatomy. Her hands, too, roamed.

By the time they dragged themselves panting and gasping and dripping from the water, neither cared about drying or about traversing the seemingly endless four or five feet to the nearest divan or even one of the lovely rugs. Kimri was fleshily padded and of sturdy farm stock just as he was. The tiled floor would not bruise her well-developed buttocks any more than it would his knees.

It did bother his toes, but he was far too busy and happy to mind the discomfort and minor abrasions.

"Hoo-*whoof!*" she gasped loudly, as he drove into her sleek wet nest of black and straight up the equally wet channel beyond. Equally wet, and considerably more slippery.

Her hands sprang to his shoulders and tugged while she clenched her rearward cheeks against the unyielding floor. She used both to push up to him with strength born of a desire to be filled to the very limits of her womb. With the back of her head flat against the floor she turned her face this way and that, wet hair trailing in glossy tendrils. Her voice trembled with the strain of taking him into her.

"Ah, ah my love—ah! M-my—uh."

"My Dove with the heart of a lion," he murmured, and drew back, nearly all the way out, and then in a lunge he absolutely filled her with himself.

He felt her nails dig into his shoulders. Still her head moved back and forth, so that her wet hair flailed the tiles. Yet she would not be a passive recipient of his lovemaking, of his fucking. She made it mutual. Her solid breasts were heaving and her eyes sparkled like wet black diamonds. She rammed those round tits into him, arching her back and whipping her hips up in unbridled passion as if trying to crush and smash her body against his, under his.

Like a fiery sword his cock cut deeply into the inner meatiness of her. He watched the darling wench's eyes cloud in lustful happiness as he filled her vaginal tunnel. Hunching broad and well-padded hips, she cradled him between them and gave herself over to the demanding totality of sexuality. Her tits, full and solid, rocked madly. Like ripe, red-brown buds ready to burst into bloom, her nipples stood above those prancing masses of breast.

He pounded in with an extraordinary display of masculine virility, the ultimate maleness. The inflamed girl met his warrior's thrusts with a happy squirming of silky, cradling hips. Stroking him and crooning now, she squirmed lustfully in whelming passion. Her movements sought more and more erogenous friction deep inside her belly. Eager and moist, its lips drooled around the stake he drove into her with almost frenzied thrusts. Grasping him, she grunted aloud at the feel of cock stretching her.

Sex-driven spike moving about within her, inside her very body, possessing her, filling her, rooting in her!

"That big th—that big thing is like, like," she gasped, "like a burning brand in me. How it heats my body—overheats me!"

Grinning at words he heard as beautiful, he sought to do more than overheat her.

I will burn her up! And he accompanied that thought with a sudden mighty flurry of action between her thighs to pound her pussy all the harder.

His new movements in her lent new enthusiasm to his fevered lover's almost frantic hip movements. The large, meaty cheeks of her ass clenched lasciviously and thrust her muscularly up at him. Sweat-wet sounds rose from the voluptuous, fleshy flopping of her tits. Equally liquid noises issued constantly around the head of his cunt-encased prick.

With surging strength, the blood-filled purple knob sank to the very heart of her churning channel, and in the instant his chest squashed her breasts and the base of his cock squashed her cunt lips as if his balls too were seeking entry, she came.

He was astonished. Her passion-gripped body began helplessly thrashing and jerking in a long series of spasms. Sweat shone on the lovely slopes and hollows of her nakedness as her womb convulsed within her. He felt its savage grabbing, all around his cock. With a squeal and a heavy shudder, she hit the pinnacle of ultimate enjoyment.

His surging, deep-thumping prick slid and sloshed through the renewed flood of lubricant that gushed through her cuntal cavern. She became wetter and wetter, looser and looser, until his raging cock seemed to fly in and out of her.

What a delight, what an unexpected delight to have fucked

her into an orgasm—and right through it!

She was nearly exhausted, he saw, going all flaccid and sagging in post-orgastic relaxation. Yet she worked on, mindful of his needs, squirming her slippery sweat-soaked body and hunching weakly to every hard, ramming drive he made into the soft slushy-wet gorge between her thighs. Then he solved her problem for her. He saw to it that she need not move and furthermore could not.

Lifting both her legs, he bent them at the knees, then pressed downward. The smooth upper surfaces of her thighs crushed down onto the swelling arcs of her breasts. Her calves dangled before his body, and with his body he crushed them down against the backs of her thighs. She was doubled up now, all cunt, a moveless package, an upturned elongated hole to be drilled while her own legs squashed her own panting breasts.

He writhed over her, pumping and shoving into that glorious aggregation of flowing desirable doubled-up curves, into the luscious channel for the housing of his cock. It was upturned now, and tightened, despite its new looseness after her spend and the juices brimming in it. Harder her breath came, and more shallowly. Her eyes bulged, staring up at him between her knees. In this straitened position what felt like a foot or two of massive and burning horse-cock drove high up her.

She trembled. She huffed in mindless ecstasy and strain. Buttock muscles tensing, he drove into her, and drove, and drove until he was gasping and trying not to cry out while his whole body tensed and lurched and heated semen left him in hard bursts. Her smile was strained as she received it. She tried her best to reach around her own doubled, upraised legs and hold him to her.

Drained and shaking, he released her legs, worked to hold himself inside her while he drew them down and alongside him. When he'd have slid aside, she grasped him,

216

holding him atop her, taking his weight—heavier, now—with pleasure. Little crooning sounds hummed up from her throat and she stroked him, stroked him while his fingers moved weakly on her and his mouth kissed the skin it was near. And she smiled.

He had risen early and fought most of the day. She had not, and she knew that many women in conquered Darum were suffering and would suffer, bereft of husbands or other protectors, sons and daughters, lovers and parents and perhaps livelihood. None, Kimri knew, was so lucky as she. Her lover slid away into a doze; she did not. She held him atop her prostrate body, stroking him and now and again pressing a kiss upon him, and she wandered about within her thoughts, and she glowed.

Drowsing pleasantly, he was brought to full wakefulness by the discreet knock at the door.

He astonished Kimri; in seconds Guy Kingsaver was beside the door with his sword all long and shining in his fisted hand.

"What is it?"

The reply was male and came in Arabic: he had brought food and drink.

"Leave it, please," Guy said in Arabic.

Waiting, he turned to grin at the naked young woman who had rolled onto one hip to gaze at him. She smiled back and pursed her lips in a long distance kiss. At last Guy opened the door, slowly and with care, sword still in fist. The corridor was empty of people, but the spiced aroma of hot, eastern food entered the room at once. She watched while he set the sword aside and squatted. Her smile broadened to a grin as she gazed at the parting of his small, tight buttocks in a way that revealed the furry bollocks slung beneath the double curve. Then he was rising, turning, and she smiled anew at sight of what he held: a good-sized wickerwork tray covered with a cloth. With a naked heel he thumped the door shut and started toward her. Instantly she scrambled to her feet and hurried to him, bare breasts jostling and swinging.

"It is not meet that you bear food to me, my hero," she said, and took the tray from him.

When she turned, his hand sprang out as if automatically to fondle her naked haunch, and she paused to receive the caress as long as he was minded to give it. At last he ended it with a slight slap, and joined her on cushions before a low filigreed table. More wondrous aromas arose when she uncovered the meal prepared for them.

They ate with appetite, for by now the sun was only a red glow and neither had had a morsel since dawn. At that, they took time to bestow an assortment of kisses and caresses on each other.

"Kimri . . . Dove," the Crusader said when his belly was full and he was minded to remain on the cushion on the floor, leaning back against a divan while merely enjoying the sensation of feeling good, of being well-fed and aglow. And in the presence of a naked, loving woman. "What a nice name your parents gave you! And yet now you have slain . . . the dove has become a lioness."

He said the words, calling her "al-Libwah," lioness, before he thought, but instantly he was sorry, for he was struck with memory. The name came into his mind, and a vision of her face: *Julanar al-Libwah.* Ah, how well and too often he remembered that fiery and noble yet vicious woman! But that she-lion was dead, dead, for all that he had probably loved her. She had loved him, he was sure. Abruptly he was sorry he had called this very different girl that, for it only made him think of Julanar when he did not want to at all. Dead of Turks, and in his arms on a bloody plain, though she had been seeking to kill him when she found her own death.

218

"You have ... gone away within yourself," Kimri, Dove, said.

"Aye," he said, and lied, for to lie was kinder: "I was thinking about how good I feel now, and how good it is to be here with you. We—" He broke off when she came near and pressed to him, kissing his shoulder. "And I was wondering, Kimri, how came you to leave your own farm and come here. And I find you in a *fruit shop?*"

She sighed, and stared straight ahead at nothing. She spoke in a low, dull voice as she remembered. "You saved me from two of the lustful warriors of Salah ad-Din, Guy Kingsaver my hero and my love. Some six weeks agone, they came again. That is, more of them came, soldiers. *Defenders of Islam,*" she added scathingly. "They were five. All five ... all had me. They slew one of my sheep, and her with milk. They forced me to cook for them, na-naked in my own home, and then they began again. Then an emir came. He punished those men, and I was gratified; again I had hope. But he took me for himself, that high noble, and my animals for the army of Salah ad-Din. Ptoo!"

Suddenly she turned her head aside and spat ritually before speaking on: "Emir Barak ibn-Yusuf made me his, but never willingly, *aiwallah!**—though in truth he was not unkind. Here, three weeks ago, he *gave* me to a man who had rendered service. My fellow Falashtimi† had seen how the wind blew and the sand stirred in our land, so he snuggled up to the Turkish overlords like a whore. He prospered, for he was their man—nay, their *boy!* He also used me as his own, but cruelly. He never knew that I laughed at him within me, for I knew him to be nothing as a lover; since I had known the best. Once. Twice, now—a tall warrior—hero of Frankistan who lately took an arrow in his chest but who sits now beside me unscathed as if in the hand of Allah!"

*"by Allah, even so!"
†Palestinian

With that she turned again to press a kiss on his shoulder, and then, hair trailing down his arm, to kiss his chest and let his nipples feel her tongue. Down her nibbling lips and tongue moved, while his hand rose to her shoulder, and then her face was in his naked lap.

"Uh," he gasped, and trembled, for she was blowing her breath lightly into his loins, riffling the curling hair there. It had only just dried from their frenetic lovemaking on the floor.

Her voice rose from his crotch in a murmur: "You have a woman?"

"I—uh—"

"I shall make you forget her!"

He smiled, looking down at the dark, dark-haired top of her head. *You are very welcome to try, my sweet dove!* Guy Kingsaver thought, but he said nothing.

She licked and stroked the soft organ, deliberately blowing her breath over it in further titillation. Meanwhile she was cupping a warm hand up under his furry balls and pressuring and pulling while she licked. In delight he listened to the wet lapping sounds of his cock's being treated so lovingly by an adoring woman.

She pressed her sweet lips over the rounded head, warmly, and worked them over it until it was slick and wet and all aglisten with her saliva. Then her jet hair caressed his thighs when she reared her head back to swipe her tongue enticingly over the very tip. Her quivering pink tongue next ducked down to lick the firming neck just under the crown of his penis.

Tremors ran up and down his thighs, rippled his muscular belly. Naturally under such treatment his somnolent organ awoke and stirred, so that her tongue had more and more area to trace over.

"Oh, it's so *pale*—such a lovely *pink!*" the daughter of the desert cooed, and he felt very intimately the breath that

220

accompanied each marveling word.

Smiling, sliding her arms around his thighs, she sucked the warm wrinkled organ into her mouth. His cock grew at once; stiffening, lengthening, swelling to fill her mouth and challenge its capacity.

"Ah," a totally delighted man gasped, and reached in under the curtain of her hair to find and fondle a softly dangling breast.

He tried hard only to cup and caress, rather than to go at once for that red-brown jewel of a nipple in its coral circle of a setting, as he wanted. What he wanted above all just now was to do nothing to stop this orally adoring darling; not to distract her from her glorious treatment of him.

Her oral ministrations had brought his penis up into a cock, a lengthy spear of hardened flesh in which the pulse beat hard. The turgid tip of that thickened staff had long since passed the rounded grip of her soft lips. It was buried in her face. Lip and tongue, she was servicing him as no woman ever had. Her hot mouth moved on him, tongue darting back and forth with wet suctioning sounds as she pulled long and deep.

His buttocks clenched and he groaned aloud. Great waves of feeling poured over him. They brought shivers to his tensing body. For a few seconds he could not help himself: he ground his crotch fiercely against her head as she slurped and pulled happily and serenely.

"Um-mmm," she said, and it was not quite a groan.

Then he controlled himself; easing off his pressure, he let the dusky darling treat him and his throbbing erection as she wished.

She fed on his cock, sucking sweetly and yet voraciously while streams of lubricant seeped, fair gushing from her yawning, yearning cunt. The oily cleft was alive with pervading desire. She reached down with a secret finger to rub herself there, then impale her own wet canal. His own pleasure soared. Her now wildly working lips and the way she pumped the passion-bloated shaft with her clinging, greedy mouth, grasping and tugging, contributed to the ever-growing intensity of his lust.

"Uh!" he gasped, stiffening and then shivering. "Ah..."

"So pretty," she enthused again, "so *pink*."

Rocking on her silken haunches, one breast lying softly and warmly across his thigh, the passion-groaning girl pumped her head almost violently up and down his staff. It jerked inside her head in tempo with the pounding of his speeding pulse. Again he gave in to impulse and moved to let his cock's broad knob burrow deeper into her hot and greedy mouth.

Clearly, intoxicatingly, he could hear her sucking up the seminal fluid that oozed freely from his enormously aroused organ. That sent a shiver through him, and his hand quivered when he stroked her mane of gleaming black hair. With a shudder he felt small pink tongue trekking fierily over him, tasting and testing the hardness and the heat of his third leg.

"Ah God's wounds," he gasped, "your tongue, God your *tongue*, woman!"

He felt her mouth clench almost furiously in happy response to his enthusiasm, milking his slickened, shining prick. He stared down at the way his cock-loving inamorata was bobbing her head over it. The sight of that glossy head working in his loins filled him with a voluptuary thrill. She was working as if to suck him up and then completely dry of the slippery juices she would drink greedily and happily down. Satin-skinned lips caressed and titillated the broad, bulging crown and long veined stalk.

She tasted the manly flavor of the fluid oozing from its rounded, delicately tinged tip, and she liked it. She made a humming "mmmm" noise, and licked, to let him know.

He listened to her swallow. He shuddered. God, but that was exciting!

"Mother of God, but you're exciting!"

He heard her response: a smug throaty chuckle.

He became aware that she was steadily moving her lower body up and down, and after a moment discovered that she was juicily riding her own impaling hand. Smiling as he realized that she was as delighted and excited as he, he commenced groping her breast with more enthusiasm, which meant more pressure. Her response was a more profound bobbing of both her head and her lower body. Eager hips shook and jiggled. Her twinned fingers ran in and out of her vagina with wet noises. She finger-fucked herself and sucked away at him in a glazed-eyed passion.

His prick quivered and throbbed with lust, increasing the girl's succulent mouthful so that her tawny face was utterly stuffed. She was obviously reveling in that fullness of her face, as well as the powerful fingers that now manipulated and twisted her breast.

He moved, just a little, and carefully.

That way he force-fed her more of his powerful tool, just a bit more, without gagging or strangling her.

Her throat accepted another quarter-inch or two. He felt that tighter, clogged channel, and the sensation wrested a groan from deep in his own constricted throat. His balls had swelled and blazed with an inner heat until they began to pain him. With the muscles of her face rippling like steel under a coating of pure dusky silk, she sucked and licked—and pumped her pussy on three of her own fingers. Her constant movements added to his delight with the shifting and rubbing of her tan, softly jiggling tits against his bare legs.

Suddenly it was there, it was necessity, and he grasped her to move strongly, surging his hips into her face. She made spluttering sounds and stroked his scrotum, tugging at the large eggs stuffing it.

"Umm, ummm-*ummm*" she hummed, jiggling all over, knowing what was happening and wanting it, wanting it—wanting to have done it.

A great shiver of tension leaped through him and in an instant his deeply contained cock jerked and sent its warm seed spurting into her mouth. "Ummmm!" She gulped thirstily and sucked for more, meanwhile moving her fingers on his balls with a milking motion. A second hard-driven spurt erupted, and a third. She could taste it, feel it shooting and bubbling into her mouth, the hot sweet thick Frankish semen she had sought, coating her tongue and sliding smoothly down her throat to warm her belly.

He collapsed back against the divan they had never used as other than back-rest. He was gasping. His eyes were closed as she changed her position, disimpaled herself, murmured, "Such a lovely *pink* cock!" and licked and licked until he had to stop her. She flowed up his body to cling to him . . .

And within a minute he was recovered enough to seize her, roughly twist her about, and impale with two big fingers that same juicy orifice from which she had so recently withdrawn three of hers.

He pumped rapidly, the heel of his hand slapping her pubis until she was moaning and jerking in passion. And more, and the fever pitch of her passion and delight crossed over into a sort of voluptuous stupor. She sprawled quaking in a sensual rapture that was almost painful while he finger-pumped her clamping, flowing cleft. She forced her own thighs as wantonly apart as she could get them and her sweaty asscheeks trembled beneath her.

He continued until she was simpering, sore, and was able to get him to stop. Then she "obeyed his command" to tickle her own clitoris, enjoying the wickedness of it whilst he

224

watched, until she was trying very hard not to scream in her orgasm.

They lay still and touching, sweaty and gasping...and in less than an hour she was kneeling on a cushion with her head and shoulders on that same divan while he groaned and strained behind her, slapping her big-cheeked ass with his hips while he fucked her hard and deep.

Eventually, *eventually* they slept.

"*The horses in their superb trappings, their bridles blazing with jewels, pranced and caracoled. . . . armor gleamed and flashed in the sun. Armorial bearings shone forth on the brightly polished shields. From jeweled helmets and from lances fluttered gloves or ribbons belonging to the ladies . . .*"

—EVA M. TAPPAN, *When Knights Were Bold,*
1911

THIRTEEN

Aftermath, With Errors

Under a blazing yellow sun and in a new plumed helmet, Guy Kingsaver of Messaria rode north, again on a personal mission for Richard the King and thus for the Crusade of Christendom.

He did not ride alone. He provided escort to Kimri, who was well and completely attired now, and happy in the saddle from which she cast frequent looks in his direction. In turn he was escorted by several helmeted men in mail whose identifying pennons fluttered from their lances. Those long poles were presently butted in their saddle-holders, so that they stood tall and slender rather than low and deadly. Now they were as flagstaffs moving across the rocky, sun-flooded land.

The horses plodded contentedly, at a walking pace. Guy had insisted that they canter for the first hour, to work any kinks out of the horses left by the previous day's strain of battle. That had been a mistake. It had enabled them to put much ground between them and Darum. That was a mistake.

"I do hate to pamper ye this way," Richard had told him this morning, "but I want this message got to Henry of Champagne as fast as possible. Whom else can I trust with its speedy delivery?"

Any number of people, Guy of Messaria had thought, but did not say. "I understand, my lord. Deukkak and I are ready. I go alone?"

"God's balls, *No*," the Lion-heart cried, looking scandalized. "With you go two knights and their squires. And ye'll not be missing any action of moment—unless of course Saladin is minded to attack us in strength. We will merely be patrolling and cleaning up this land hereabouts; securing Darum's environs. And Guy—is it your wish that girl you fetched in last evening should be taken to the safety of Tyre?" Richard's smile was tinged with a trace of slyness. "I mean, she may not have been special, but she is now, hmm?"

"Thank you, lord King. Aye. Kimri is a good woman, bereft of family and farm by the Turks she hates as much as we do. I shall miss her, but she has no place here in Darum, and even less when we again take to the field. I should not want her among the . . . camp-followers."

"I would like to see all the camp-followers dry up in the sun and blow away on this accursed Outrémer wind!" Richard's face reddened and went worse than serious during that hot outburst. Then, calmly and with a twinkle in those cornflower eyes: "But—you shall miss her, you say? Holy Mary, Guy, how many nubile young women have you had in this land, here and there awaiting you, with impatience?"

Guy Kingsaver flushed, and had no answer. Surely that so many women and girls awaited him here and there was not his fault, and surely the king knew it. Things just . . . happened.

The king did know it, and the youthful hero's flush and uncomfortable look earned him a royal clap on the shoulder that would have staggered many men.

"I did not mean for you to consider and make answer, you irresistible Cypriot devil! Now I do want you also to stop at Castle d'Entremont, Guy. Convey my greetings to the Knights of the Hospital there and apprise them that one more town is Saladin's no more. Advise good Aimar Neversmile that those Hospitallers with me still acquit themselves better than well and bravely, and all are alive and in possession of good right hands. Night with them if you will; he will certainly make invitation. Just do not expect any such quarters as you enjoyed yester night—or any such activity, either!

"God speed, Guy Kingsaver. Your *escort* will be ready to depart within the hour. Ah—and hie thee back to me, my brave squire!" That was dismissal, but the king had another thought: "Oh—find that doubtless dear girl some clothing. Take what you want from the coffers of these women we captured with the keep—they are Turkish doxies anyhow. Though I must say I found one last evening who loves buggery—not to mention remaining alive, and free!"

And Guy went away from the king, who was beset by decisions and orders to be issued. The Crusader was glad to have discovered that Richard had not been celibate on the night of another victory. One of Richard's secretaries handed Guy the despatch to Count Henry/King Henry. Guy tucked it away with care. Just under an hour later, the six of them rode from Darum in a northeasterly direction, at the canter.

He and Kimri and their escort were well out of sight and earshot when the great cavalcade approached Darum, from the northwest. Bugles and horns and drums announced their approach before they were in sight. Soon the blazing banners of Burgundy and Champagne and the Kingdom of Jerusalem clearly identified the leaders of that army. It was mostly French. Duke Hugh and Count Henry had arrived in gorgeous panoply at last—the day after Darum's fall.

Richard made no mention of how many men might still be alive had they been more timely in their arrival. He greeted them right heartily, with an embrace for Henry, whom he deliberately called "King." Richard also saw the

229

excellent opportunity for pomp and celebratory festivities, which he did love. He at once announced a grand dinner and fête for that evening, and set men in charge of its preparation.

At about noon, in the presence of thirty and more other barons, he made the announcement that Darum was to be part of the Kingdom of Jerusalem, as a belated wedding gift of the King of the English, the Temple of St. John, *and* of Austria to King Henry and Queen Isabella.

No one dared object. Indeed, a cheer arose. Despite the fact that he had not been consulted, Leopold managed not to look unhappy. It was, as Anselm the Templar and Richard had agreed beforetime, too fine and noble a gesture for any to quibble or even raise an eyebrow, much less opposing voice.

Not until an hour or so past noon did Richard think or see opportunity to ask his nephew why he and Burgundy had led their force in from the northwest rather than by the main route; the supply route.

"Ah! That brings bad tidings I hoped to spare you for a day or so," Henry said. "We received positive knowledge that somehow Castle d'Entremont was taken by the Saracen. I knew that if I led my men down—"

"D'Entremont! The Hospitallers' keep—the Invincible Castle? No! By God's balls—no!"

"Aye," Henry said, perhaps wondering at Richard's almost extreme reaction. "I feared me that if I were to lead my men down that road and we looked up to see the yellow banners of Saladin flying over d'Entremont . . . we'd all want to lay siege, and might not reach you for a month. We must have the castle back—it commands our main supply route! Yet retaking it will be far from easy. God alone knows how the Paynim succeeded in taking the place."

Richard swung away. "Riders! I want hard men and fast

horses to ride at full gallop..." He trailed off, looking up at the sky and the position of the sun. "Nay. Too late, too late. They even left so nobly at the canter! Ah Satan gnaw my bones—I have sent Guy Kingsaver to certain death!"

Grove Press Victorian Library